MEET ME UNDER THE MISTLETOE

JACKIE BRAUN

Copyright © 2008 by Jackie Braun Fridline

Originally published as The Tycoon's Christmas Proposal by Harlequin Romance.

All rights reserved.

No part of this publication may be reproduced, distributed, or transmitted in any form or by any means, including photocopying, recording, or other electronic or mechanical methods, without the prior written permission of the publisher, except as permitted by U.S. copyright law. For permission requests, contact Jackie Braun Fridline at authorjackiebraun@gmail.com.

The story is a work of fiction. All names, characters, and incidents portrayed in this production are fictitious. No identification with actual persons (living or deceased), places, buildings, and products is intended or should be inferred.

CHAPTER ONE

Dawson Burke was used to people doing things a certain way. *His* way.

For that reason alone, he was annoyed at the message he'd just retrieved from his voicemail. He tapped his cellphone against his chin as he stared out the limousine's windows at the bumper-to-bumper traffic fighting its way into Denver. What did Eve Hawley mean she would be *popping by* his office later today to discuss his gift needs? What was there to discuss?

He'd only met with his previous personal shopper on a handful of occasions during the past several years. Most of his dealings with Carole Deming had been accomplished by phone, text or email. Dawson provided a list of names and the necessary compensation. In return, Carole bought, wrapped, and saw to it that his gifts were delivered.

No muss, no fuss. Mission accomplished. Everyone was happy.

Well, he wasn't happy at the moment.

In her message, Eve said she needed to ask him some questions about the intended recipients on his list. Eve said she preferred to meet with her clients face-to-face at least once before setting out to do their shopping. Eve said it gave her a feel for their tastes and helped her personalize the purchases she made.

Eve said...

Dawson scrubbed his free hand over his eyes and expelled a ragged breath. This was the third voicemail full of questions and requests that he'd received from the woman. He didn't have time to deal with this bossy stand-in any more than he cared to make time for Christmas. He couldn't help but wonder what had possessed Carole, who was recuperating from knee surgery, to suggest this woman as her replacement. Maybe he should call her and see if she could recommend someone else. Someone who didn't ask unnecessary questions. Someone who simply did his bidding and required no handholding along the way.

The limousine pulled to the curb in front of the building that housed the offices of Burke Financial Services. His grandfather, Clive Burke Senior, had started the company, which specialized in managing stock portfolios and corporate pensions. Clive Senior had been gone nearly a dozen years and Dawson's father, Clive Junior, had retired the spring before last. These days, Dawson was the Burke in charge. And he believed in running a tight ship.

His secretary rose from behind her desk just outside his office the moment the elevator doors slid open on the seventh floor. Her name was Rachel Stern and the moniker suited her perfectly. She was an older woman with steel-gray hair, shoulders as wide as a linebacker's, and a face that would have made a hardened criminal cross to the opposite side of the street before passing her. In the dozen years Rachel had been in his employ, Dawson couldn't recall ever seeing her crack a smile. Stern. That she was, but also efficient and dedicated. Sometimes she seemed to know what he wanted even before he did.

This morning was no different. She fell into step beside him, prepping him on the day's itinerary even before he had peeled off his leather gloves and shrugged out of his heavy wool overcoat.

"The people from Darien Cooper called. They got held up in traffic on their way in and are running about fifteen minutes late. I've put the information packets in the conference room and the PowerPoint presentation is ready to go."

"And my speech for the Denver Economic Club this evening?" he asked.

"Typed, fact-checked, and a copy is on your desk. The local stations are looking for a preview since their reporters won't be able to get anything back before the late-night news airs. I've taken the liberty of highlighting a couple of points that might make for good sound bites."

"Excellent."

"Oh, and your mother called."

Dawson gritted his teeth. He reminded himself that the only reason she called him so often was because she loved him and was worried about him. Of course, that did nothing to assuage his guilt. "Does she want me to call her back?"

"No, she just asked me to remind you to have your tuxedo dry-cleaned for the ball this weekend. She's reserved a seat for you at the head table and won't take no for an answer."

He bit back a sigh. The annual Tallulah Malone Burke Charity Ball and Auction was the see-and-be-seen-at event for Denver's social elite. He'd hoped to send a generous check along with his regrets. But the ball was celebrating its silver anniversary this year, and he had little doubt that his mother would show up at his door to personally escort him if he dared decline.

The cause was worthy, raising funds for the area's less fortunate. At one time, Dawson had been happy to do his part by suiting up like a penguin, shaking hands, and making small talk with Denver's movers and shakers. But for the past few years he'd made excuses not to attend the event, which always fell the second

Saturday after Thanksgiving. It was a bad time of the year for him. The absolute worst, in fact. He'd been grateful that his mother, who was a stickler for appearances, had been willing to let him shirk his responsibilities as a Burke. Apparently, his amnesty had run out.

And she claimed he'd inherited his stubborn streak from his father.

He consulted his watch. "My housekeeper should be in by now. Give her a call. Ingrid will see to it that the tux gets cleaned. And when you get a minute—"

"A cup of coffee and a toasted bagel, light on the cream cheese, with a side of fresh fruit." Rachel finished for him.

"Please."

His efficient secretary could all but read his mind, whereas Eve Hawley apparently was unable to make sense of a simple list of names, even when it included particulars like sex, age and how they were acquainted with Dawson.

"Will there be anything else?" Rachel asked.

"Actually, yes." He retrieved the phone from the inside pocket of his suit coat and handed it to her. "Call Miss Hawley back for me. Hers is the third number down. She's the personal shopper Carole recommended. Tell her I'm too busy to see her today and, although it should be *completely* self-explanatory, see if you can answer the questions she claims to have about the list of names I had you email her last week."

"Very well." She sounded as enthusiastic about the task as he'd felt.

"Thanks." He reached up to massage the back of his neck as he said it, grimacing when pain radiated all the way down his spine. It had been a frequent visitor the past three years, ever since the car accident that claimed the lives of his wife and daughter. Tension made the pain worse. This time of the year, when memories and regrets swirled their thickest, it became almost unbearable.

"Is your back bothering you again?" Rachel inquired in a tone devoid of the syrupy concern he so detested. The last thing he wanted was to be the object of pity. Yet he knew that's precisely what he had become in many people's eyes.

Poor Dawson Burke.

"A little."

"I'll call Wanda and see if she can come in for a session between your afternoon meetings today," she said, referring to the masseuse he'd kept on retainer since leaving the hospital after the crash.

That sounded like heaven, but he shook his head. "No time. Nick Freely called while I was on my way home last night. I promised to squeeze him in today and go over some new stock options with him."

Freely was a top-tier client. The firm managed several million dollars in assets for him, which meant he got preferential treatment, even if it meant shoehorning in an appointment on a fully booked day.

"I can call him, reschedule," Rachel offered.

"No. I tell you what. Ask Wanda to come by my house this evening. That way I'll be nice and limber for my speech."

When Rachel was gone, he made a mental note to increase the amount on her holiday bonus check. She had it coming. His very efficient secretary was worth every penny.

Eve Hawley had something coming, too, he decided that evening. And it wasn't monetary compensation.

He was lying on the portable table his masseuse had set up in the center of his den, only a thin white sheet standing between him and immodesty, when his housekeeper tapped at the door.

"Excuse me, Mr. Burke," she said from the doorway. "There's someone here to see you."

He wasn't expecting company. He had barely an hour before he was due to leave for his speech. As Wanda kneaded his knotted muscles with hands that would have done a lumberjack proud, he asked between gritted teeth, "Who is it?"

"Eve Hawley."

He lifted his face from the donut-shaped rest and gaped at the housekeeper. "She's here now?"

"Yes."

The woman was relentless and obviously incapable of doing the job if, even after talking to Rachel earlier today, she was still hounding him.

"Tell her I'm indisposed."

"I did, Mr. Burke. But she's insisting on seeing you," Ingrid said.

"Insisting? Well, if she's insisting..." He figured he knew a sure-fire way to get rid of her. "Send her in."

"Right now?" The housekeeper gaped at him.

"Yes. Right now." If Eve Hawley wanted to see him, Dawson would make sure she got an eyeful.

Ingrid's gaze cut to his bare back and the sheet that rode low across his hips, covering the essentials and then leaving his legs exposed. She was old enough to be his mother. In fact, it was at his mother's suggestion that he'd hired her. Her pursed lips told him exactly how inappropriate she found his suggestion. But, like all—or at least the vast majority of the people in his employ—she minded her own business and did as he asked.

"Very well," she said, withdrawing from the room without further comment.

"Carry on," he told Wanda, before lowering his face back into rest. The masseuse was working her way down his spine when he heard the door open a moment later. The person who entered sucked in a startled breath. Although it was small of him, Dawson grinned at the floor.

"Oh. You're..."

"Busy," came his muffled reply.

Feminine laughter trilled. "Actually, I was going to say naked."

"Not quite." But he frowned at the same floor he'd smiled at a moment earlier. She didn't sound nearly as distressed by that fact as he'd hoped she would be.

"I'm Eve Hawley."

"Yes, I know," he said crossly. "Even if my housekeeper hadn't announced your arrival, I would recognize your voice from the numerous messages you've left on my phone."

"Messages that you have failed to return," she had the audacity to point out.

"They were returned. My secretary called you back," he said.

"Ah, yes. Mrs. Stern. If I'd wanted to talk to your secretary, Mr. Burke, I would have dialed her directly. I need to speak to you."

Dawson felt the muscles in his back beginning to tighten again despite Wanda's competent ministrations. "Look, Miss Hawley, surely Carole Deming briefed you on what I'm looking for. This is gift shopping, not rocket science. If you can't do the job—"

"Oh, I can do the job. I just believe in doing it well," she replied in a voice that was stiff with pride.

Another place, another time, he might have admired it. But he had no patience for it at the moment. "I won't take up much of your time," she promised.

Dawson relented with a sigh, but he didn't raise his head from the padded hole. He was being rude, insufferably so. But then that was the point. The woman had already strained his patience.

"Fine. Shoot."

"You want to discuss this right now?" Her tone was uncertain.

"Right now is all the time I have. My schedule is very tight and will be for the next several days. This is precisely why I employ a personal shopper. I don't have time to do it myself."

That wasn't the whole truth, but it was the only explanation he planned to give this annoying woman.

"I see." He thought she might object and leave. That had been his goal. But he heard a pair of heels click over the polished wood floor. They stopped just outside his limited field of vision.

"I have some concerns," she said, her tone that of a professional who apparently was not the least bit concerned about discussing business with a nearly naked man. Perhaps like the housekeeper, she, too, was old enough to be his mother.

"What are these concerns?"

"Well, in addition to business associates and acquaintances, your gift-giving list includes friends and several family members."

"My parents, sister, her husband, and their two children," he said. "I'm well aware of who is on the list, Miss Hawley. After all, I'm the one who wrote it." Well, his secretary had done that, but he'd approved the final version.

"I do things a little differently when family members are involved."

Heels clicked on the floor again and Dawson was forced to revise his opinion of her age when a pair of lethal-looking stilettos came into view. They were red and made of faux alligator skin. But those weren't the reasons that had Dawson subtracting a few decades from her age. Women of his mother's generation generally didn't have little butterflies tattooed on their ankles.

Curiosity got the better of him. He brought his elbows up and levered part way off the table so that he could see her. Then he sorely wished he hadn't. The rest of Eve Hawley, from the curves that filled out her knit dress to the long dark hair that waterfalled over her shoulders, was every bit as sexy as her legs and those shoes. Suddenly, the fact that he was nearly naked didn't give Dawson the advantage he'd sought. No, indeed. That had shifted squarely to the black-haired beauty who, at the moment, was eyeing him with her arms crossed, brows raised, and unmistakable amusement glimmering in her eyes.

He sent a glance over his shoulder in the direction of his masseuse. "Wanda, that will be enough for now."

"I don't know, Mr. Burke. You still feel awfully tense to me," she objected.

Out of the corner of his eye, he thought he saw Eve's full lips twitch.

"I'm fine." To Eve he said, "Give me fifteen minutes and we'll go over your concerns."

"Happy to."

This time he was positive she was holding back a smile before she turned to saunter from the room.

Eve waited in a sitting room that was tucked just off the kitchen. The housekeeper had thoughtfully brought her a cup of hot tea. She sipped it now as she stared into the flames of the fire that was flickering cheerfully in the hearth and contemplated her client.

Dawson Burke was a surprise, and not because he'd been clothed in nothing more than a bed sheet at their introduction. He was not the paunchy, middle-aged workaholic who so often relied on her services. God bless those men since they had been helping to pay her bills for nearly a decade, but she hadn't expected Dawson to be quite so young or so handsome or—she sipped her tea—so physically fit.

As an unattached woman of thirty-two, there was no way details such as those were going to escape her attention.

Eve was relatively new to the Denver area and the state of Colorado, for that matter. The beauty of her job was that she could do it anywhere. She'd been looking for a fresh start after a particularly nasty breakup the previous spring, and after some online research she'd decided that anyplace with a view as pretty and panoramic as the one the Mile-High City boasted just might provide it.

So, she'd been settling in, building up a client list, and slowly sinking down roots. She'd caught a lucky break when she'd met Carole Deming while shopping in a boutique a couple of months earlier. The two women had hit it off right away. The fact that Carole was fifteen years older and they were technically competitors hadn't stood in the way of their friendship. Indeed, Carole had been kind enough to toss some of her clients Eve's way while she recuperated from surgery.

What was it she'd said about Dawson Burke? "I think you'll find him a challenge."

At the time, Eve had assumed Carole was referring to his gift needs, not his personality. Now she suspected she understood perfectly why the other woman had laughed while saying it. A challenge? Just getting past his pit bull of a secretary had taken considerable effort, which was why she'd decided to drop by his home unannounced.

Eve didn't mind difficult clients. She'd worked for plenty of them in the past, picky people who gave her carte blanche to buy presents for others or clothing for themselves only to veto her every choice later. But this was different. She simply couldn't do what Dawson wanted her to do without gaining more insight. It wasn't right. As far as Eve was concerned, family members deserved more thought when it came to gifts. She had no qualms about buying for them, but she wouldn't allow the purchases to be impersonal.

She set the tea aside and stood, walking closer to the fire when memories left her chilled. Her mother had died when Eve was eight years old. Suicide had been rumored at the time, but officially, her death had been ruled a drug overdose. Regardless of the cause, her mother's family had blamed Eve's father. Growing up, she'd been shuttled from one relative's house to another's, while her dad had hit the road, ostensibly to try to turn his pipedream of being a musician into a bona fide profession. More accurately, though, he'd been running from a reality he could not accept.

The last she'd heard he had a gig at a pub in Myrtle Beach. At sixty-two, Buck Hawley was no longer waiting for his big break. But he was still running.

He'd missed out on more than two decades of Eve's life, though he had always managed to send her a gift to mark another birthday and Christmas. She hated those gifts. They were always impersonal things that Eve knew upon opening he hadn't picked out. For that matter, even the signatures on most of the cards hadn't been his.

While growing up that had wounded her. All these years later it still hurt. She'd needed her father's time, craved his attention. Absent those, at the very least, she'd wanted to know what he thought about her while picking out her gifts. So, when clients asked her to buy for their loved ones, she required more than the name and age and sizes that Dawson had provided on his list.

"Would you care for more tea?"

She turned to find the man in question standing in the doorway. His dark hair was combed back from his forehead, lean cheeks freshly shaved. He was wearing an expertly cut charcoal suit with a white shirt and conservatively patterned tie, yet her heart did the same little somersault it had upon seeing that muscular back.

"No, thank you."

He nodded. "Well, not to rush you, but I do have someplace I need to be. I believe you said you wouldn't take up much of my time."

"Right." She retrieved her oversized bag from the side of the chair. "I do things a little differently than Carole does."

"So I gathered," he replied dryly.

"For starters, when I shop for close relatives such as those on your list, I need to know something about them." He opened his mouth, but before he could speak Eve added, "Something beyond their sex, age, sizes, and your price range. For instance, what are their hobbies? Do they have a favorite color? Do they collect something? For the children, are they into video games, sports? Who's their favorite recording artist? I don't believe in gift cards, fruit baskets, flower arrangements or the like. Anyone can purchase and send those. They don't take any effort or require any thought. I won't buy gifts like that."

"Maybe I have the wrong person for the job."

Dollar signs flashed in neon green before her eyes. This was a big account, the biggest by far of the ones Carole had fed her. The commission it was likely to bring would go a long way toward fattening up the bank account her cross-country move had depleted. Still, Eve crossed her arms, blinked the dollar signs away, and said, "Maybe you do. It's a matter of principle for me. I can't do my job well without that information."

He studied her a long moment before sighing. "What do you need?"

Eve pulled a folder from her bag, which she handed to him. "Given how difficult it's been to reach you, I decided that instead of conducting an interview I would give you this questionnaire. Fill it out at your convenience, but if I could have it back to me by next Monday, that would be great."

"Anything else?"

She didn't miss the sarcasm in his tone, but she chose to ignore it. "Actually, there is. While I don't mind flying blind when it comes to buying gifts for business associates and clients, if you have any insights or personal anecdotes about any of the people on your list, I'd welcome them. Feel free to jot down anything that comes to you on the line I've provided next to their names."

"Maybe I should go shopping with you."

Again, she ignored his sarcasm. Smiling sweetly, she replied, "It's kind of you to offer, but that won't be necessary. Unless you really want to, I mean. I can always use someone to carry the purchases out to the parking lot."

She wasn't sure why she had just baited him, other than the fact that his arrogance rubbed her the wrong way.

"Excuse me, Mr. Burke?" the housekeeper said from the doorway. "The driver has brought the car around."

"Fine." He turned his attention back to Eve. "I believe we're finished."

"For now," she allowed, and had the satisfaction of watching him scowl.

CHAPTER TWO

Dawson prided himself on being the sort of man who thought outside the box when finding solutions for problems. It was one of the things that had helped make him a success in business. So, when adversity knocked Friday afternoon, he let opportunity answer the door.

"Your mother is on line one and Eve Hawley is on line two," Rachel buzzed to tell him.

"I'll take the call from my mother. Tell Miss Hawley I'll call her back." As he said it, he glanced in the direction of his inbox, where the questionnaire she gave him remained untouched. He had a good idea of the reason behind Eve's call. He also knew why his mother was phoning. The charity ball was Saturday. The lesser of two evils, he decided.

"Hello, Mom."

"Dawson, darling. How are you?" she asked.

"Fine."

"So, you always say," she chided. "But I still worry about you."

"There's no need to, really."

But she disagreed. "It's a mother's job."

"I'm an adult, Mom. Thirty-eight last month," he reminded her.

"Your age doesn't matter. Nor, for that matter, does mine." Tallulah was quiet for a moment. Then, "I know this is a difficult time of the year for you."

"Mom—"

But she spoke over him. "It's a difficult time of the year for everyone. We all miss Sheila and Isabelle."

Hearing the names of his late wife and daughter turned his voice unintentionally crisp, "Don't. Just... don't." He softened the command with, "Please."

"Dawson—"

But he held firm, even if he did moderate his tone. "I prefer not to talk about them. I've made my wishes very clear."

"What is clear," Tallulah began, "is that you've locked yourself inside a prison of your own making for three very long years. You've always been a fairly rigid individual. But in that time, you've become overly controlling, overly driven. You don't make any time for friends or family, let alone yourself. You spend every waking hour at the office."

"Yes, and Burke Financial has thrived as a direct

result," he replied. "The last quarter's earnings were the best in the company's history."

"Your father and I don't give a damn about the business," she snapped. The fact that his mother had used even a mild oath had Dawson blinking in surprise. This was a woman who rarely raised her voice let alone lost her temper. Neither had ever been necessary. She'd always had more effective ways of getting her children to toe the line. She pulled out one of the big guns now. "I hate to say this, Dawson, but I'm very disappointed in you."

He sank back in his chair and closed his eyes. Whether he was eight or thirty-eight, that particular weapon never failed to hit the mark.

His tone was contrite when he said, "I'm sorry you feel that way, Mom. That's certainly not my intent."

"I know." But, of course, she wasn't through. "Have you made plans for the holidays?"

It was a Burke tradition to gather for dinner at his parents' estate on Christmas Eve. In fact, that had been his destination the evening of the crash. Ever since then, he hadn't been able to make it. Physically, mentally, he just couldn't go there on that day. Even on other days, driving that particular route reopened a wound that had never fully healed. He expelled a ragged breath. "You know that I have."

"San Tropez again?" she inquired. Dismay was obvious in her tone.

He'd gone to that tropical paradise each Christmas for the past two years, unable to remain in snowy Denver for the anniversary of that fateful night. This year, however, he'd decided on a different destination. "Actually, I thought I'd try Cabo. I've rented a condo on the ocean until just after the new year."

Like San Tropez, Cabo San Lucas was warm and sunny with gorgeous beaches and, most importantly, no one who knew him. People wouldn't ask how he was doing, tilting their head to one side in sympathy as they spoke, or regarding him with an overly bright smile that failed to camouflage their pity.

"Alone?" his mother asked.

"Mom—"

But she continued before he could get more out. "You know, it wouldn't bother me so much that you refuse to spend the holidays with loved ones in Denver if I at least knew you were spending them with someone special."

"I'm fine." He repeated.

But she threw him a curve. "Are you seeing anyone, Dawson?"

"I've gone out a couple times," he admitted. The dates had been unmitigated disasters, from the stilted conversations at the beginning to the awkward goodnight kisses at the end. Both attempts had left him feeling guilty and angry at fate all over again. He didn't see any reason to divulge that information to his mother, however.

She apparently figured it out, because she said in a plaintive voice, "Oh, son, at some point you need to move on with your life."

"I have," he insisted.

He got up each day, didn't he? He went to work. He'd turned the company into an even bigger success than it had been under his father.

As usual, though, his mother cut to the chase. "But you haven't forgiven yourself."

No. He hadn't forgiven himself. He couldn't do that. He closed his eyes, only to see it all happening again. He'd been the one behind the wheel of the car on that snowy Christmas Eve, the one firmly in control of all their destinies until a patch of black ice had changed everything.

After the impact with the bridge abutment, Dawson was the only one to survive. He'd walked away with a nasty gash on his forehead, a back injury and a busted arm. His wife had died instantly, while his young daughter had hovered on the brink for several more hours with internal injuries before a surgeon had come out of the operating room to deliver news Dawson still wasn't ready to accept.

"I'm very sorry, Mr. Burke. We did all we could, but we couldn't save her."

Grief and guilt had literally taken him to his knees that day, and they had remained his constant companions ever since. The gaping holes in his life, in his heart, were simply too big to fill, even if he had any inclination to do so. Dawson couldn't forgive himself.

His mother's voice tugged him back to the present. "I want you to be happy," she said.

He opened his eyes before giving them a rub with his free hand. She didn't get it. No one did. For him, happiness had ceased to be relevant.

"Don't worry about me, Mom," he told her for the second time.

A long pause ensued. When his mother spoke again, her tone was suspiciously nonchalant. "When I was in the city last week, I ran into Mary Harrison. Her daughter was with her. You remember her daughter, Kaitlyn. Lovely girl."

His mother's tone as much as her words set off an alarm bell in his head. He silenced it by saying, "Do you mean the one who got married a few years ago and moved to California?"

"Yes, but she's divorced now, poor thing, and recently moved back to Denver." The alarm sounded a second time as his mother continued. "She still has that same bubbly personality. She'll be at the ball tomorrow evening. I was thinking of asking her to sit with us. That would give us an even number at our table. And you know how I like an even number."

Leather creaked as Dawson shifted uncomfortably in his chair. This was the last thing he needed. The last thing he wanted.

"Mom, I would really prefer you didn't do that."

"Nonsense. Kaitlyn is very nice, dear. You'll both have a good time. It doesn't have to lead to anything. In fact, I'm not sure she's ready for a relationship yet. Her divorce was final only a few months ago. But at least it will give you both an opportunity to get your feet wet again." Sounding pleased with her plan, she added, "I'll phone her after I hang up and invite her."

He couldn't believe it. His mother wanted to set him up with a newly divorced woman who was probably every bit as unenthusiastic about the matter as he was. The event might be a charity ball, but he wasn't a charity case.

"No!" He slammed his free hand down on the desk blotter with enough force to make a loose paperclip jump.

"Dawson?" She sounded hurt.

"Sorry, Mom."

"It doesn't have to be a real date. Just two friends spending an evening together," she suggested.

He picked up the paperclip and took out some of his frustration by bending it in half before tossing it aside. It landed atop Eve's questionnaire in his inbox and inspiration struck. Perhaps there was a way he could kill two birds with one stone.

"I know you're trying to help, and I appreciate it,

honestly. But there's no need for you to call Kaitlyn. As it happens, I already have a date."

Eve was on her way to Boulder, the rear of her Tahoe already laden with the morning's finds in Denver, when her cellphone trilled. She answered it on speaker so she could keep her hands on the steering wheel. Dawson Burke's authoritative voice boomed through the vehicle's interior.

"Mr. Burke, this is unexpected."

He sounded confused when he asked, "Didn't my secretary tell you I would be calling?"

"Mrs. Stern? Yes, she did. Which is why I'm in a state of shock. I mean, if I had a dollar for every time your secretary has told me you would get back to me..." She let her words trail off.

"Very funny," he muttered. "Are you this flippant with all your clients?"

"Nope. You seem to bring it out in me." But she moderated her tone to add, "Thank you for returning my call."

Even if the call in question had been a couple of hours ago.

"You're welcome."

"The reason I phoned you earlier is that I'm on my way down to an art gallery in Boulder to pick up some pieces by a local artist for another client of mine. Buying artwork for someone is like buying clothes. It has to fit the recipient's style."

"Which makes it personal," he said.

"Exactly. So, I was wondering if art might be something that would appeal to any of the friends or family members on your list?"

He made a humming noise. Then, "My parents' walls are pretty full at this point, and I wouldn't presume to know my sister's taste in art as she's made a hobby out of redecorating her home every few years. As for my friends on the list I gave you, I don't know."

"Well, it was just a thought." Her exit was coming up, so Eve shifted her vehicle into the right lane. "How's the questionnaire coming along?"

She heard him clear his throat. "Actually, I wanted to talk to you about that."

"You haven't filled it out," she guessed.

"Not yet, no."

"Mr. Burke—"

"Dawson, please."

"All right. And you may call me Eve. But I really would like that information. To do my job well, I need it, as I explained to you the other night," she said.

"It's a matter of principle, I believe you said."

"That's right."

"And if I refuse?" he asked. The question sounded almost like a dare.

The dollar signs flashed again, but Eve thought about her father and remembered her own disappointment. She couldn't knowingly perpetuate that kind of heartache on someone else. Her tone was firm when she replied, "I'd have to ask you to find another personal shopper. So, are you refusing?"

"No, but I have a better idea," he said. "Do you have plans for tomorrow evening?"

"As a matter of fact, I do." Since moving to Denver, Eve had spent nearly every Saturday night alone. But as it happened, she did have something going on. She'd told Carole she would stop by with Chinese food, a bottle of wine and some Christmas movies for the pair of them to watch.

"I see." Then he surprised her by asking, "Would it be possible for you to change them?"

Her curiosity was good and stoked. "Why? What do you have in mind?"

"Each year around this time my mother throws a really big to-do. Perhaps you've heard of it? The Tallulah Burke Charity Ball and Auction."

She put on her blinker and maneuvered the Tahoe onto the exit ramp. "No, sorry, but I haven't been in Denver very long."

"That's all right. Stick around and you will." The pride in his tone was unmistakable when he added, "It's been an annual event for the past twenty-five years, drawing in the well-heeled and well-connected to raise money for the area's homeless and women's shelters."

"How nice," Eve said and meant it.

"Yes, well, the party is tomorrow night."

Comprehension dawned and something that felt like interest danced up her spine, even if Eve didn't want to admit it. After all, the man wasn't her type at all. Too arrogant. Too brooding. Too rigid. "Are... are you asking me out?"

"Not exactly," he said. "I need an escort for the evening. And you will be compensated."

Indignation blasted along with the horn of the car behind her, and she realized she'd come to a full stop even though she had the right of way. She sent the other driver a wave of apology and turned into the nearest parking lot.

"Eve?"

She waited until she had shifted the vehicle into park before she let loose. "Maybe I wasn't clear about the nature of the services I provide. I'm a personal shopper, not a personal anything else."

She heard Dawson cough. Actually, he sounded as if he might have choked a little, which suited her just fine. He deserved it.

"I'm sorry. I didn't mean to imply otherwise. Compensation was a poor choice of words. What I meant by it was that many of the people on my gift list will be in attendance. In addition to my parents, sister and her family, a number of business acquaintances and longtime Burke Financial clients attend."

"Oh."

It was on the tip of her tongue to apologize when he added, "I thought seeing them, meeting them, might help you do your job more effectively. You know, live up to those high principles you speak of."

"Are you mocking me?"

"No." He expelled a breath. "For the record, Eve, I admire you for taking a stand. I haven't met many people in business whose principles can hold up under pressure from the bottom line."

He sounded sincere, which went a long way toward soothing her temper. "So, this would be sort of like a business function."

"It would be *exactly* like a business function," he corrected. "But with better food. No rubber chicken or cheap champagne. My mother doesn't believe in doing anything halfway."

As Eve was privy to Dawson's hefty gift budget, she decided it was a trait he had inherited.

"It sounds very fancy."

"Black tie required." He cleared his throat. "Do you have something appropriate to wear?"

"I think I can find something suitable in my closet," she lied smoothly. If she said yes, she would have to do a little shopping for herself. "Where and what time?"

"Does that mean you'll come?" He sounded surprised, maybe even relieved.

She was probably going to hate herself for it later, but she said, "Yes."

"And your other date? I trust that the last-minute change in plans won't cause any problems."

Eve nearly laughed out loud when she realized that he thought the plans she'd mentioned earlier were with a man. She had enough pride not to enlighten him.

"Don't worry. I can reschedule it. I mean, this thing with you is work, after all."

CHAPTER THREE

Dawson cursed and yanked at his bowtie as he stood in front of the vanity mirror. This was his third attempt at tying it and the stupid thing remained lopsided. He wasn't sure why his fingers wouldn't cooperate, any more than he could identify the origin of the nerves churning his stomach.

He hadn't felt amped up before either of his previous dates, disasters that they'd become. And his evening with Eve wasn't a date at all. It was a business function. He finally managed a symmetrical bow and, satisfied with his appearance, called for his driver to bring the car around.

Twenty minutes later, business was the last thing on his mind when Eve opened her apartment door. She was a vision in red with her full lips tinted the same dangerous shade. She'd done something different with her hair, pulling that dark wavy mane up to reveal the slim line of her neck. A pair of diamond studs winked on her earlobes as she tilted her head to one side and regarded him with a smile that he was pretty sure dated back to the original Eve.

"Hello, Dawson."

"You look…" Words failed him. For a moment, he thought his heart might fail him, too. The woman standing before him should come with a cardiac arrest warning.

"This works for the occasion, right?" She did a three-hundred-and-sixty-degree turn that made him wish he had a defibrillator handy. "I wouldn't want to stand out."

"You'll stand out, but for all the right reasons," he replied, with more honesty than he'd intended.

Her smile bloomed again. "That's quite a compliment. You look pretty good yourself. It's a sin there are so few places for a man to wear a tuxedo nowadays."

"I doubt you'll get many men to agree." He pulled at his collar as he said it. The damned thing seemed to have grown too tight.

Eve laughed. It was a husky sound, entirely too provocative for the mere reason that it wasn't intended to be. "Come on, a tuxedo can't be as uncomfortable as my shoes. My arches are going to hate me by the end of the night."

Dawson allowed his gaze to skim down, which he

regretted almost immediately. He'd already known she had a pair of killer legs. Tonight, they were accentuated by strappy black sandals that added a good three inches to her already respectable height. His pulse took flight alongside the little butterflies tattooed on her ankle. He didn't particularly care for the reaction. Business, he reminded himself.

"Ready to go?" he asked. "While I have no problem arriving fashionably late, my mother is a stickler for punctuality."

"Ah. Right. So, exactly what have you told her about me?"

"Your name."

"A man of few words," she said with a laugh. "Just let me get my coat."

He glanced around while she did so. Her apartment was a loft in a former commercial building that had been converted to residential use. Its exposed ductwork, distressed wood floors and battered brick walls gave it an almost industrial feel. It was small, its total square footage probably not equal to that of his master suite, but Eve certainly had made the most of every inch.

Her taste was as bold and uncompromising as the woman. Vivid colors were splashed against neutrals and a rather eclectic mix of artwork adorned the walls. At the far end of the room, he spied a slim staircase that led to the sleeping loft. A horizontal metal railing defined the space up top and allowed a tantalizing glimpse of a platform bed beyond. He saw more bold colors there, rich crimsons, plums and golds. For a moment, he allowed himself to wonder what one might interpret from her decorating choices.

"Dawson?"

He turned to find her standing directly behind him. She held a small clutch in her hands and was already wearing her coat, a long wool number that was cinched in at the waist with a belt. Even covered up with not so much as a scrap of red showing, she still exuded far too much sex appeal for his comfort.

He glanced away and cleared his throat. "Nice place you have here."

"Thanks. I like it."

"Excellent location given your job." He made a circular motion with one hand. "Close to shops and all."

"Yes." She smiled. "But work wasn't the only reason I chose it. I like being in the thick of things."

She would. Even though he didn't know her very well, he'd already figured out that Eve was the sort of woman who grabbed life with both hands and refused to let go even when the ride got wild. Maybe especially then.

"Well, we should be going."

As Dawson followed her out the door and waited for her to lock the deadbolt, he wondered why he felt both eager to leave and disappointed that they couldn't stay. When they arrived at the Wilmington Hotel twenty minutes later, he had the answer to half that question. He hated affairs such as this.

The hotel's amply proportioned ballroom could accommodate several hundred guests. Only a fraction of that number had arrived yet, as it was early, but most of his family was there. His mother spotted them from across the room as soon as they cleared the door. She motioned to him to join her, but he sent her a wave and steered Eve in the opposite direction, where, handily, the bar was. He needed a little fortification before he faced his mother and the rest of his family and began fielding their questions. He also needed to bring Eve up to speed on a few pertinent facts.

"How about a glass of wine?" he suggested.

"I suppose that even though this is technically a work function for me, a nice glass of Chardonnay wouldn't be out of line," she replied.

"Not at all," he agreed.

When they reached the bar, he ordered wine for them both.

Eve took a sip as she glanced around.

"I guess you weren't kidding when you said your mother doesn't believe in doing things halfway. I wasn't expecting the party to be quite this large. This room must be set up for at least a few hundred people to dine."

"More than five hundred, actually. The room can

fit seven hundred, but my mother thinks it feels too cramped when it's at capacity."

Eve blinked in surprise. "Is everyone in Denver on the guest list?"

"Sometimes it feels that way," he said. He swept an arm out to the side. "But what you see here are the people with the deepest pockets. My mother's specialty is getting them to reach in, grab a wad of bills, and make a donation."

"She sounds like a formidable woman," Eve said.

He merely smiled. His mother could indeed be that, he thought, recalling the previous day's conversation. At times, Tallulah was relentless.

"So, is your family here yet?" Eve inquired, taking another sip. "I'm eager to meet them."

"Some of them are." He cleared his throat then. "Before I introduce you, though, I need to ask a favor of you. I would prefer that they didn't know what it is you do for a living."

"Ashamed of me?" She tilted her head to one side, sounding more amused than insulted, although he thought he saw vulnerability flicker briefly in her dark eyes.

"Of course not. It's just that I don't want them to feel..." He groped for the right word.

"Like you brought in a designated hitter to size them up because you couldn't be bothered to shop for their gifts yourself?" She smiled sweetly.

His conscience delivered a swift kick to his

nether region, and his manners slipped. "You know, you can be annoyingly blunt at times."

Far from insulted, she laughed. "It's a gift."

"Maybe you should sign up for a Dale Carnegie course."

His annoyance gave way to amusement when she replied, "I already took one. Passed it with flying colors, as a matter of fact. A star pupil." She smiled at him over the rim of her glass. "So, who exactly do they think I am?"

Dawson felt as if he had been dumped back into junior high school when he admitted, "Actually, they think you're my date."

"Ah. Your date." She was enjoying his embarrassment. Of that much, he was sure. "And how long have you and I been an item?"

"We are *not* an item." He was back to being annoyed.

"First date. Got it." Eve nodded. "I'll try not to be too obvious when I'm peppering them with questions to get an idea of their likes and dislikes."

"You won't be the only one with questions," he replied distractedly as he caught sight of his mother homing in on them with the precision of a heat-seeking missile. She didn't even stop to chat with the people who greeted her along the way. There would be no avoiding her this time.

He put his arm around Eve's shoulders and

leaned close to whisper, "My mother is headed this way."

"Uh-oh. Should I bat my eyelashes at you or something?" she asked.

"This is a bad idea," he mumbled, not quite sure if he felt that way because of her glib reply or because he'd caught a whiff of her perfume. It was sexy, sinful. He ignored the tug of awareness it inspired and pasted a smile on his face as his mother reached them.

"Dawson!" Tallulah called. "I thought I saw you come in a moment ago."

He kissed her cheek. "Hello, Mom. You look as radiant as ever. Is that a new dress?"

"It is, though I doubt you care," she replied with a chuckle, letting him know that his attempt at flattery had not sidetracked her in the least. Speculation lit her eyes even as her lips curved into a gracious smile. "And who might this lovely young woman be?"

Eve knew she was being inspected from head to toe even if Tallulah Burke smiled as she acknowledged her. Dawson performed the introductions.

"Mom, this is Eve Hawley. Eve, my mother, Tallulah Burke."

He looked uncharacteristically uncomfortable afterward. All of his usual cockiness seemed to have evaporated. He was a powerful man. A very handsome and powerful man. One who was used to bending others to his will. But at the moment,

Dawson Burke was merely a son, who obviously loved and respected his mother. Eve liked him all the more for it.

"Eve, it's very nice to meet you." Tallulah shook Eve's hand, covering it with both of her fine-boned and heavily bejeweled ones. She didn't let go immediately afterward. She held on and pulled Eve a little closer as she added, "I have to say, I was a little surprised when my son mentioned yesterday that he would be bringing a guest to the party this evening. I wasn't aware he was dating anyone. I guess the mother is the last to know."

Even as Tallulah said it, Eve got the feeling that very little got past the woman. This was no flighty society maven. Her blue eyes were keen with intelligence and, at the moment, a great deal of curiosity.

"Eve and I haven't known one another very long," Dawson hedged.

"Oh?"

"This is actually our first date," Eve supplied. She didn't quite bat her eyelashes at Dawson, but she came close. Dawson scowled.

"Really? How did the two of you meet?" Tallulah asked, her gaze never wavering from Eve.

"A mutual friend got us together." Since it wasn't exactly a lie, Eve had no problem supplying the information.

Out of the corner of her eye, she saw Dawson nod, apparently pleased with her response. Then, before his mother could probe any further, he added, "It's no one you know, Mom. More like a business acquaintance."

Someone called her name then. Tallulah waved in their direction before saying, "Well, I need to mingle. You should do the same, Dawson. It's expected."

"Of course."

Tallulah turned to Eve then. "I'll look forward to getting to know you better over dinner."

Will I measure up?

The question had Eve's stomach knotting and some of her old insecurities managed to sneak in, despite the fact that her relationship with Dawson wasn't the romantic one they had led his mother to believe.

"Something tells me the salmon won't be the only thing grilled here tonight," she murmured once she and Dawson were alone.

"Don't worry. My mother is harmless."

Eve decided to reserve judgment. Admittedly, her first impression of Tallulah was a positive one. The woman seemed kind, and the very fact that she threw an annual ball to raise funds for charity elevated Eve's opinion of her. But Eve had had enough negative experiences in her past to know better than to trust first impressions.

Pot calling the kettle, she thought, since making a stellar first impression was important to her.

Thanks to her penchant for sniffing out sales and spending her pennies on quality pieces, Eve knew what to wear. She also had no problem holding her own in social settings. One of the great aunt's she'd lived with had been a stickler for etiquette. Eve knew how to sit with her legs crossed demurely at the ankle. She knew how to walk with her chin up, shoulders back. She knew which fork to use for the various courses served at dinner. And when it came to the art of small talk, she could hold her own with the best of them.

But she was a fraud. An absolute and utter fake underneath all of her props and polish.

She had not been born into money, and, as she'd learned with her last boyfriend, Drew, when it came right down to it, for some people it was the pedigree that made all the difference.

Eve notched up her chin, slid her arm through Dawson's, and in her best high-society voice, asked, "Shall we go forth and mingle?"

He heaved a sigh. "I'd rather not, but yes. Just let me do most of the talking."

"Oh, don't worry about me. I'm a regular chameleon," Eve assured him. "No one will ever suspect that I don't belong here."

He sent her a questioning look, which she ignored. Despite those noxious self-doubts, she continued to smile brightly.

As they canvassed the room for the next half

hour, everyone with whom they stopped to chat seemed surprised to see Dawson and oddly tongue-tied around him, as if they were afraid they might say the wrong thing.

At first, Eve thought it was because he exuded power. A lot of people, regardless of their social standing, found that intimidating. But it was more than his importance. She felt an undercurrent, something just below the surface of the polite conversations that seemed almost like sympathy. It didn't make sense. Why would anyone feel sorry for Dawson Burke? The man had it made. High-powered job, wealth, exceptional good looks, and a body that appeared to have been chiseled from granite. Yet for all that, she reminded herself, he couldn't manage to find a real date for an evening.

"I'm curious about something," Eve began as they made their way over to the tables where the items for the silent auction were displayed.

"Hmm?" he replied absently.

The first item they came to was a gift basket full of aromatherapy bath products. The opening bid was far more than the actual value of the individual components and yet several others had already topped it. Dawson scrawled his name down along with an outrageous amount. She added "generous" to his list of attributes.

"I'm trying to figure out what's wrong with you," Eve stated bluntly.

He set the pen down and straightened, regarding her from beneath furrowed brows. "Excuse me?"

"Well, you're obviously successful and you're attractive. Built, too," she added, giving one of his biceps a teasing squeeze through the sleeve of his tuxedo jacket. "Even your penchant for lavender-scented bubble baths doesn't detract from the decidedly macho vibe you've got going."

"It's for charity," he replied dryly.

"Right." She winked, but only because she knew it would annoy him. The man seriously needed to lighten up. And for some reason, she had appointed herself the one responsible for seeing that he did. At least tonight.

"Charity," he muttered a second time.

She conceded with a nod. "Still, given all that, why couldn't you get a real date for tonight?"

Dawson looked perplexed by the question. "Aren't you having a good time?"

Surprisingly, Eve was and so she admitted as much. "All things considered, I am enjoying myself. I'm just, you know..." She motioned with her hand. "Curious."

"Curiosity killed the cat, Eve."

She merely shrugged. "Cats have nine lives. So, why aren't you dating anyone?"

"Who says I'm not?"

She settled a hand on one hip. "Everyone we've met tonight seems shocked to see you out at a social function." She paused for effect before adding, "Especially in the company of a woman."

"I have a very demanding position as the head of Burke Financial." It was a weak excuse, and he apparently knew it based on the way his gaze slid away after he said it.

"Okay, got it. Work is the love of your life, so you have no room for a flesh-and-blood woman," Eve deduced, being purposefully blunt.

His gaze returned to hers. "I enjoy what I do, Eve. There's nothing wrong with that."

"I agree wholeheartedly." She crossed her arms. "I enjoy my job immensely, too. I mean, hello? I'm paid to shop. A bad day hunting up just the right item beats a bad day chained to a desk, even in a corner office in a high rise with incredible views."

"Of course, you enjoy your job." Dawson snorted. "Name me a woman on the planet who doesn't like to shop?"

Even narrowed her eyes. "Got a pen and fresh notepad handy? The list is very long, which is why I've remained gainfully employed twelve months of the year since I started doing this nearly a decade ago. Not everyone who hires me is male or in need of someone to buy their holiday gifts."

Indeed, a lot of people, male and female, delegated all their wardrobe decisions to Eve.

His smile was tight when he conceded, "Point taken."

"Actually, my point is that while there's nothing wrong with liking what you do for a living, you also need to enjoy, well, living. That's hard to do when what goes on at the office sucks up nearly every waking hour."

He frowned and said nothing, but for just a moment, when she'd spoken about enjoying life, his expression had turned grim and almost haunted. She'd struck a nerve, of that much she was sure. Which nerve, however, remained a mystery.

They moved to the next item up for auction. When Eve saw what it was, she squealed in delight. Two tickets to the stage production of Les Misérables. Its limited run at the Denver Center for the Performing Arts was scheduled to come to an end just before Christmas. The set of seats being auctioned were prime, a fact that was reflected in the most recent bid. Even so, she snatched up the pencil and jotted down a sum that topped the previous one by twenty-five dollars.

Dawson was rubbing his chin when she straightened. "Your line of work pays very well."

She laughed ruefully. "I'll be eating salad for a month, but I'm dying to see this show again."

"Again? How many times have you seen it?"

"Six. And I watched the movie starring Hugh Jackman and Anne Hathaway four times, although I didn't like it as much."

"Let me guess. Russell Crowe's Javert ruined it for you."

She shook her head. "I didn't mind his performance. In fact, I thought some of the reviews of him were unfairly brutal. It's just that Hollywood can't inspire the same, I don't know, feeling as watching a live stage performance."

"Which is why you want to see it again," he said.

"Exactly. Tickets for seats this good are impossible to get at this point. Believe me. I've checked. And checked. And checked."

He tapped the paper with the tip of his index finger. "Well, if you really want them, you're going to have to bid higher than that."

"You think?" She nibbled her lip, mentally reviewing her budget to see where else she could skimp.

"I know. The evening's young yet and the people with the fattest wallets tend to arrive fashionably late to these things. You can always buy the soundtrack," he added.

"I already have the soundtrack."

On cassette tape, a CD, and all available music platforms for iPhone. She listened to the score so often she could sing every song from memory. But to see *Les Mis* again? Live and in person? And in those prime seats? She sucked a breath between her teeth and before she could change her mind, she leaned over to scratch out her first bid and up the amount by fifty dollars. Afterward, she sent him a weak smile.

"I like salad and I've been meaning to lose a few pounds anyway."

His gaze took a lazy detour down her torso, lingering on her breasts and then the curve of her hips, before returning to her face. His brows rose right along with her pulse rate. Even though he didn't say a word, his eyes communicated something quite clearly. Eve knew that look. It was rooted in sexual interest. Her heart knocked out a couple of extra beats in response since that sexual interest was hardly one-sided.

What was wrong with her? He was her client. Besides, she wasn't sure she even liked Dawson Burke. Of course, like and lust weren't mutually exclusive, making this attraction all the more inconvenient.

Dawson's shoulders lifted in a casual shrug and his expression turned aloof and arrogant once again, leaving her libido feeling duped.

They moved on. Standing before the next auction item was a couple Dawson apparently knew well.

"Hey, look who's here." The man smiled as he reached out to clasp Dawson's hand.

"Hi, Tony. Christine." He leaned over to buss the woman's cheek. "It's been a while."

"That's because you haven't returned any of our phone calls," Tony reprimanded lightly.

Apparently, he made a habit of that, Eve thought.

"We've been worried about you," Christine added.

Dawson cleared his throat as he sent a fleeting glance in Eve's direction. "There's no need to worry about me."

The couple followed the direction of his gaze, spied Eve and attached a far different meaning to his glance.

"So I see. I'm happy for you, Daw," Christine said. "Very happy."

"Yeah," her husband added. "It's about damned time you returned to the land of the living."

Because he hadn't actually introduced her, Eve did the honors herself. She recognized their names from Dawson's gift list, so she discreetly sized them up during the brief conversation, trying to concentrate on the kind of item that might suit their tastes, ignoring their curious comments, which Dawson had made quite clear did not warrant follow-up questions.

"Well, we probably should make our way to the head table," he told her, winding up the conversation just after Christine mentioned running into the parents of someone named Sheila at the theater recently. "It was nice seeing you both again."

"Yes. We'll be having our annual party weekend

after next. The invitations go out on Monday. Do you think you might make it this year?" Tony asked. "And, of course, Eve is welcome to come, too." He sent a smile in her direction.

Uh-oh.

But she was saved from having to answer. Dawson was shaking his head. "Sorry. Other plans."

"Oh." Tony nodded, although he was clearly disappointed. "Maybe we can get together for dinner one night between Christmas and New Year's. Christine and I have been meaning to try out that new steakhouse that opened downtown."

"Sorry," Dawson said again. "I'll be in Cabo from Christmas Eve until the first of the year."

"Cabo?" Tony glanced at Eve and then back at Dawson. "I guess I thought that maybe this year…" His words trailed off awkwardly.

"We should head to our table, too," Christine said, taking her husband's arm and sending an apologetic smile in Dawson's direction. "It was nice meeting you, Eve. I hope we'll see you again."

Although it was the other couple who moved away, Eve was left with the distinct impression that Dawson was the one who had retreated.

CHAPTER FOUR

"Dawson?"

He blinked twice and seemed to snap out of whatever fog he'd been in. "Yes?"

"You mentioned something about taking our seats," Eve reminded him.

"Right." He put a hand on the small of her back, guiding her away. He didn't sound irritated, just weary, when he said, "I think I've done all of the mingling I can stand."

The head table was at the front of the ballroom just to the right of a raised stage, presumably for easy access to the podium and microphone. The table was round and had place settings for eight. A woman with two young boys was already seated there. The boys were slouched down in their chairs, looking sullen and subdued, but their expressions brightened considerably when they spied Dawson.

"Uncle Dawson!" they squealed in unison.

"You're here!" the older one said.

To which the younger one added, "Mom bet Dad that you'd find an excuse not to show up, even though you promised Nana you'd come this year."

"You're not supposed to tell him that," the other boy said, rolling his eyes in disgust.

"Why not? It's true."

"You're so lame."

"Boys, no name calling," the woman Eve assumed was their mother warned. Then she said, "Hello, Daw."

"Hello." But he returned his attention to his nephews. "Nice suits." Like all of the men in the room, the boys were outfitted in black tuxedos. The only difference was that their ties were askew and their white shirts were wrinkled and coming untucked. Eve found them adorable.

"Mom made us wear them," the younger one grumbled, pulling at his collar.

"I know how you feel." Dawson laughed. He put his hand behind Eve's back and drew her forward. "I'd like you to meet my guest, Eve Hawley. Eve, these are my nephews, Brian and Sean. Brian is six and Sean is eight."

"I'm seven, Uncle Dawson," Brian corrected.

"And I turned nine over the summer. Remember? You couldn't make it for dinner, but you sent me that chemistry set." The way Sean's mouth twisted on the words told Eve exactly what the boy thought of the gift. Carole must have been off her game. Eve would have to be sure she got him something awesome this time around to make up for it.

"Ah. Right. Seven and nine," he repeated, nodding and looking slightly embarrassed. Was that because he'd forgotten their ages or because the gift had obviously been such a dud?

"Well, it's nice to meet you both," Eve said and she meant it. She was determined that by the end of the evening she would have a good idea of the kind of gifts they would cherish from an uncle they clearly adored. An uncle who had clearly been absent from their lives lately.

Before she could ponder why, the boys' mother asked, "Aren't you going to introduce us, Daw?"

She had to be his sister. She shared his dark coloring, with the added bonus of having their mother's startlingly blue eyes. She was a striking woman—a striking woman who at the moment was regarding Eve curiously.

"I don't know that I should," he said. And Eve wasn't at all sure he was joking.

"Fine, then I'll do it myself." The woman stood and smiled at Eve. "I'm Lisa Granderson, Dawson's much-better-mannered sister."

"It's nice to meet you, Lisa."

That seemed to be Eve's stock phrase this evening and the evening was young yet. When she had agreed to accompany Dawson, she'd known she would be meeting a lot of people, in particular people who were important enough to him to rate being on his gift-giving list. But honestly, she had a feeling her brain was going to explode before the night was over. She had a pretty good memory, but it would certainly help if she could take notes. Trying to remember all these names and personalities was going to prove difficult.

The other woman studied her for a moment, sizing her up. Eve felt herself brace, and those old insecurities threatened to rise to the surface. But all Lisa said was, "I love your dress. That color looks incredible on you." Her gaze slid to Dawson. "Don't you agree?"

"Yes, incredible," he said stiffly.

"Thank you," Eve murmured.

"Why don't you sit next to me?" Lisa invited. "We can talk fashion and you can tell me how you were able to drag my reclusive brother out of his cave for the evening."

"Sorry. Mom has the seating arranged," Dawson said before Eve could respond. Picking up a small place card, he told his sister, "Eve is next to Sean. It looks like Mom's put you between Dad and David." He glanced around then. "Speaking of your husband, where is he?"

"He and Dad are out by the coat check." Lisa rolled her eyes when she added, "They're watching the last period of the hockey game on David's phone."

"The Avalanche are playing the Red Wings," Sean supplied.

Dawson snorted as he shook his head. "Does Mom know what they're doing?"

"What do you think?" Lisa said.

"I think if she catches them, there's going to be hell to pay." Dawson laughed after saying it. The sound was a bit rusty at first, but it wound up rich and inviting.

His reaction surprised Eve. She hadn't been aware the man knew how to smile, let alone give in to mirth. Apparently, she wasn't the only one in shock. Everyone seated at the table had turned to him. But it was his sister's expression that caught Eve's notice. Lisa looked…hopeful?

"I've missed you," she said, her eyes turning bright. "I'm so glad you came tonight, Daw."

He unbuttoned his jacket and tucked his hands into the front pockets of his trousers. Though his shrug was intended to be casual, Eve saw the discomfort he tried to hide. "You know Mom. She wouldn't take no for an answer since this is the silver anniversary of the party and all."

"Well, whatever the reason, I'm glad you're here. And it's good to hear you laughing again," Lisa said.

Dawson glanced Eve's way, but then his attention was diverted by an older man, who slapped his back before pulling him in for a bear hug.

"Dawson! You made it."

The man was the same height as Dawson, although his build was a little thicker and less muscled. He was handsome, distinguished in the way men got from the same crow's feet and silver hair that women paid big money to diminish and conceal. Eve would have figured out his identity even if Dawson hadn't said, "Hello, Dad. How are you?"

"Better now that you're here."

Was Dawson the black sheep of the family? The prodigal son returning? Given all the comments, Eve couldn't help but wonder.

"So, what's the score of the hockey game?" Dawson asked.

The older man shook his head in disgust. "The Avalanche are down by two. They should have traded that goalie when they had the chance."

"Actually, they're down by three now," inserted a younger man Eve assumed was Lisa's husband, David. "Detroit just scored during the power play."

At this, Lisa stood. "That's it." She settled one hand on her hip and held out the other. "Give me your earbuds before Mom gets to the table and pitches a fit." She nodded in Eve's direction then. "And before Dawson's date gets the impression that his family is completely backward."

"Dawson has a date?" David asked as he handed over the contraband.

"Yes, he does." This came from Tallulah as she joined them at the table. Eve felt her stomach knot. And that was before the woman smiled brightly and said, "Why don't you introduce Eve to your father and David, Daw, and then we can all sit down and start getting better acquainted."

After he made the introductions and they took their seats, Tallulah said, "Eve, dear, why don't you tell us a little bit about yourself?"

Eve worked up a smile as she straightened in her seat. "What exactly would you like to know?"

"Anything you wish to share. This isn't an inquisition, dear." Tallulah laughed, intending to put her at ease.

"No, that comes later," David inserted *sotto voce*. Lisa slapped his arm and the boys giggled. Dawson's expression softened.

"Why don't you start with where you're from?" Tallulah said. "I detect an accent of sorts in your speech."

"Actually, I was thinking the same thing about all of you," Eve replied without missing a beat. Then she added, "I'm from Maine originally. I was born in Bangor. I guess to folks here it probably sounds as if I flatten my vowels."

"Maine? You're a long way from home," Tallulah commented.

"Do you have family here?" Lisa asked.

"No. No family here." At least she didn't think so. But her father tended to get around. In college she'd gone into a Daytona Beach bar while on Spring Break only to discover her dad was the opening act for the band.

"What brought you to Denver?" Dawson's father asked.

"I came here for the view." It was mostly true.

"That's an interesting reason to pull up stakes and move across the country," he replied.

She gave a delicate shrug. "I was ready for a change of scenery."

"What about a job?" his father asked. "Did you have something lined up here?"

"Not exactly, but I had no problem finding employment once I arrived."

"What line of work are you in?" his mother asked.

Eve felt Dawson's foot nudge hers beneath the table. He needn't have worried. She'd told him she wouldn't lie and once again she didn't have to. "I specialize in sales," she said.

"Well, if you ever need any investment advice, go see Daw. He's got the Midas touch when it comes to picking stocks." Tallulah beamed with pride.

For the next several minutes, while his family subtly grilled Eve, she returned the favor. And not just for work purposes. They were an interesting bunch, likable, too. Despite their obvious curiosity about her, they were warm and inviting. They were not at all what she'd expected. Given Dawson's wealth, she'd figured his family for upper crust—emphasis on crust—and she'd been prepared for them to be distant or to act superior. Drew's family had been outright judgmental of those who came from less affluent families.

The Burkes, however, were anything but.

Dawson was turning out to be a surprise, too. There was far more to the man than first met the eye, which was saying a lot given how little he'd been wearing at their first meeting.

Initially, Eve had pegged him as a workaholic, the sort of man who was too busy even to buy gifts even for his family. Then she'd thought maybe he was a self-absorbed CEO, indifferent to everyone around him and estranged from his loved ones.

But now, she wasn't sure. His family obviously adored him and even though he wasn't overly demonstrative, it appeared the feeling was mutual. Why then did he have to be "dragged out of his cave," as his sister had put it?

"Eve?"

He'd leaned in close to say it and when she turned to reply, her cheek brushed his. They both drew back at the brief contact.

"Have you come to any conclusions?" he whispered.

"No," she admitted. Then blinked. "Oh, do you mean about gifts?"

He frowned. "Of course, I mean gifts. What did you think I was referring to?"

She shook her head and worked up a smile. His personal life was none of her business. He was a client, nothing more. And she was at this event to find out more about the people on his list, in particular the members of his family.

"Nothing," she replied. But because he was still frowning, she added, "I might not have actual gift ideas in mind, but I'm definitely getting a good idea of the personalities of the recipients, and that will provide a good jumping off point."

Tallulah took the stage then to welcome everyone and introduce the minister of a local church who said the blessing. Having re-established her priorities, Eve made polite conversation with the adults and began to subtly pump Dawson's nephews for information about their hobbies and extracurricular activities. By the time the salad plates were being removed to make way for the main course, she was pleased to have already come up with some excellent leads.

Dawson's mind kept wandering, which was odd since he prided himself on his laser focus. But while the wait staff brought dishes laden with pork tenderloin, grilled salmon, chicken marsala and an assortment of steamed vegetables, rice, and boiled red-skinned potatoes to each table, he was only half-listening to his father's lament over the Fed's decision to raise the interest rate a quarter point. He found much more fascinating the discussion Eve was having with his nephews about video game strategies.

She was talking them through level six of what was apparently one of the hottest games among prepubescent boys, if his nephews' reactions were any indication. Brian and Sean were absolutely enthralled.

Dawson was, too. But in his case, it had less to do with her tips on how to defeat a dragon and secure extra lives than the effect her laughter was having on him. This may be a job for her, but she obviously liked kids.

Eve glanced up and caught him staring. "What?" she mouthed.

He shook his head and mouthed back, "Nothing."

How could he tell her that he hadn't expected someone who looked as glamorous as she did to be such a natural with children?

She would probably be insulted, even though he considered it a compliment. A lot of women he knew weren't overly fond of kids. Even his late wife hadn't been comfortable around children. Oh, she'd adored their daughter, and Dawson had been close to persuading Sheila to try for a second baby just before the accident. But she hadn't been the hands-on sort, preferring to relinquish what she called "the minutiae of child-rearing" to their nanny. That had been a source of friction in their marriage, since their opinions of what constituted minutiae differed greatly.

Like Sheila, Dawson had grown up with every advantage and luxury at his disposal thanks to his parents' wealth. But while his mother had been practical enough to delegate certain responsibilities such as cooking, cleaning and, at times, carpooling to the hired help, she'd been integrally involved in all aspects of her children's lives.

That hadn't changed even though they'd grown up and moved out. Across the table, he heard his sister and mother arguing over the current length of hemlines.

"There's nothing wrong with showing a little more leg," Lisa said.

"If you're young and have long, slim legs like yours or Eve's, no," Tallulah agreed. "But women my age or who have put on a few too many pounds, shouldn't show so much skin. It's not attractive."

She dabbed demurely at her mouth with her napkin. His mother could be very old-school when it came to certain things. For instance, she still abided by the no white before Memorial Day or after Labor Day fashion rule that Lisa insisted was outdated.

"You could show a little more skin for my taste,"

Clive inserted, sending his wife of forty years a bold wink.

Tallulah wagged a finger in his direction. "Stop flirting with me in front of the children."

Laughter erupted. Eve joined in. Dawson did as well. Afterward, his chest ached. He'd missed this, he realized. The good-natured bickering, the teasing, the laughter.

He'd always been the most serious of the Burke bunch, a trait his father claimed had skipped a generation and came directly to Dawson from Clive Senior.

Grandfather had been an imposing man, downright rigid in some ways. Dawson's father had called the older man Sir until the day he died. Perhaps that was why Clive Junior insisted his own children call him Dad and his grandkids call him the more informal Gramps. So, the comparison to Clive Senior wasn't exactly a compliment. These days, Dawson supposed, it was more apt than ever.

He glanced around the table at the smiling faces of his family and then at Eve. She was smiling, too. Looking radiant, lovely, so vibrant and… alive.

For the first time since the accident, Dawson's regret was not that he hadn't died, but that he had forgotten how to live.

CHAPTER FIVE

After the meal was finished and the servers began clearing away the dishes, Tallulah once again took to the stage. This time, as she stood at the podium, she reminded her guests why they had come.

"Thanks to your past generosity, a lot of lives have been changed for the better this past year. I know I can count on that generosity again tonight. The silent auction will close in another hour. If you aren't lucky enough to take home one of the incredible items supplied by our various sponsors, I encourage you to consider making a donation.

"In the meantime, please enjoy yourselves. We have a wonderful DJ, Dan Williams, on hand. So, let the dancing begin."

After Tallulah exited the stage to applause, the music began to play. The DJ kicked off with a slow number in deference to the fact that people had just finished their meals. Dawson leaned back in his seat, biding his time. Another hour or so and he could leave, his duty to his family fulfilled as well as his duty to Eve. Surely by then she would have enough information to do her job.

She had turned sideways in her seat so that she could see the stage. Now that the music was playing, one of her feet had begun to tap in rhythm with the beat. The polite thing to do would be to ask her to dance. His mother was giving him pointed looks in that regard. But he didn't. Dancing would require entirely too much physical contact with this woman for his comfort.

Of course, he should have known Eve wasn't the sort of woman who would wait to be asked. Bold, he thought again, when her gaze locked with his and her full lips curved in a smile.

"Do you dance?"

He made a dismissive sound. "It's been a while."

And it had. The last time Dawson had been on a dance floor, he'd been in this very room. With his wife. While their daughter slumbered safely at home under the watchful eye of a sitter. The realization caused him to frown.

"No need to look so distressed," Eve assured him, misinterpreting his pained expression. "I hear it's like riding a bike. You never forget how."

"I'm not—"

But she was already rising to her feet.

"Come on. It will be fun."

Fun? Right. He doubted that. But his family was watching, his mother nodding in approval, his sister's eyes growing misty again. He couldn't protest without disappointing them.

"Very well." He bit back the accompanying sigh.

"Try not to look so tortured," Eve quipped as she grabbed his hand and led him to the dance floor.

He and Eve were the first couple there. The only couple, he realized with a quick glance around. They might as well have had a spotlight shining down on them. The music made it too loud to hear, but Dawson imagined the murmurs coming from the crowd as he took Eve in his arms.

In addition to feeling conspicuous, he felt wooden and awkward as the past and the present intertwined, making way for comparisons that he didn't particularly like. Sheila had been petite, her build small and delicate. Eve was tall for a woman and her heels made them nearly the same height. He rested one palm just above her hip and grasped her hand, determined to keep a respectable distance between his body and her dangerous curves.

As soon as they began to move to the music, however, that space began to evaporate. Thighs mingled. Their hips bumped. Sheila had been pliant in Dawson's arms, going in whatever direction he chose. Not Eve. It was clear almost immediately that he was not the one in control.

A tendril of her hair tickled his nose when he turned his head to whisper, "You're leading."

"Yes, I am." She said it without a hint of apology. Then she asked sweetly, "Do you have a problem with taking direction?"

"A problem? No. Not really. I simply prefer to give it." He attempted to back away, but the scent of her perfume followed right along with the rest of her. Before he knew it, she was close enough to his body that he swore he could feel the vibration when she made a tsking sound.

"And here I thought you were original, Dawson. But that's such a typical male response. It's a good thing I'm wearing high heels or I'd be drowning in testosterone."

"Funny."

Eve executed a turn that Dawson wasn't prepared for and he stepped on her toes. She grimaced.

"I should apologize for that, but I find myself wanting to say it serves you right. I'm a far better dancer when I'm allowed to take the lead," he said meaningfully.

"Funny. I feel the same way."

That had him frowning. "Do you mean to tell me you always lead?"

"For the most part. You could say it's a habit." Her shoulders lifted in a delicate shrug that seemed at odds with her iron will.

"Just what kind of men do you date that leading while dancing has become a habit for you?" he asked.

"The kind who are secure in their manhood," she replied. She leaned back as she said it. Amusement glittered in her dark eyes. She knew she had him. There wasn't much he could say in response to that without impugning himself.

Dawson exhaled slowly and shook his head. He felt irritated, frustrated and, heaven help him, invigorated. "You're something else."

"Thank you."

"I'm not sure I intended that as a compliment."

"No? Well, that's all right." She brought her cheek close to his and he felt her breath caress his ear when she added, "I'm going to take it as one anyway. Lemons from lemonade, that's my motto."

Dawson gave in and let Eve lead for the rest of the song. It was either that or he was going to continue to knock knees with her and step on her toes. He preferred not to make an even greater spectacle of himself, even if it meant handing over control.

Thankfully, by the time the song ended, they weren't alone on the floor any longer. Several other couples had joined them, including his parents. Clive and Tallulah were smiling at him. He could only imagine what conclusions they were reaching, especially when, as another slow song started, Eve was still in his arms.

"Care to do this again?" she asked. She sweetened the deal by adding, "I'll be good and let you lead."

Because he felt just a little too tempted, he shook his head and released her. "Maybe another time."

They stayed at the ball for another hour and a half, which was long enough to hear the results of the silent auction. Eve didn't win the theater tickets, but then Dawson had known that her bid, generous though it was given her means, ultimately wouldn't be enough. Indeed, the winner had outbid her by nearly five hundred dollars. This was for charity, after all.

"Oh well," she said when the winner was announced. "I've got the soundtrack."

"Maybe you can listen to it while you dine on lobster," he said, referring to her earlier mention of having to eat salads if she won.

But she was shaking her head. "Lobster? I'm from Maine. Once you've had it there, where it's caught in the morning and on your plate that afternoon, you're pretty well spoiled. I'll have a steak. A nice, juicy T-bone cooked so rare that it melts in your mouth."

His own mouth began watering when she made a

little humming noise. To his mortification, her benign talk of red meat was whetting far different appetites. He glanced at his watch. It was just after ten. He was relieved that the evening was almost over, and not just because of his unexpected attraction to Eve.

Even though the point of bringing her had been to introduce her to his family and some of the other people on his Christmas list, he wasn't sure he appreciated the way she'd been received. Everyone liked her. That shouldn't have come as a surprise. She was a likable woman, not in spite of her outspoken nature, but because of it. But it was more than that. He saw the speculation in their gazes and read between the lines in their comments. He knew what they were thinking: he had finally moved on with his life.

Nothing illustrated this more than his mother's question while he and Eve were saying their goodbyes.

"Will you be coming to dinner tomorrow afternoon?" Tallulah inquired.

Sunday dinner with his parents was a tradition, or at least it had been until the accident. He, Sheila, and Isabelle had rarely missed. In the intervening years, however, he could count on one hand the number of times he'd shown up.

So, he shrugged. "I don't know, Mom. I have a lot I want to wrap up."

Tallulah nodded, not quite able to hide her disappointment. "Before you leave for Cabo."

He swallowed. "Yes."

She forced a smile to her lips and sidled closer. "Well, if you change your mind, I hope you'll bring Eve. She's delightful, Daw."

He cleared his throat. "It's not what you think, Mom. Eve and I aren't... serious."

"No? Well, maybe you should be."

Dawson thought about his mother's remark during the ride home. Eve was seated next to him on the limousine's plush leather seat. She was wrapped up in her long wool coat. Even so, the scent of her perfume kept drifting to him, just as it had on the dance floor. It was sexy, dangerous. It slipped over and around him and cinched like a lasso. He found it only a small consolation that the woman was completely unaware that his insides were being trussed up like a rodeo steer. She was talking business.

She had grabbed some paper hand towels from the dispenser in the women's bathroom before they left, and was now jotting notes down on them.

"I couldn't help but notice your mother's jewelry. She's obviously very fond of gemstones."

He snorted at the understatement. As far as he knew, it was his mother's one weakness. "If it sparkles, she's got to have it."

"There's a boutique in town that carries one-of-a-kind pieces from a Venetian artisan. His work is quite remarkable and of the highest quality. I was in the shop last month to purchase something for another client and remember seeing some lovely rings. I'll pay him a visit first thing Monday and let you know what I find."

She shifted in her seat, undoing the top button of her coat and loosening the silk scarf beneath it. Her perfume wafted to him and once again had him thinking about sex—the act itself and how long it had been since he'd engaged in it. He would work out when he got home. Thirty minutes on the treadmill and another twenty with the free weights should do it. Followed by a cold shower, he amended when she began to suck on the end of her pen.

"Okay," he managed.

"As for the boys, that's easy. They're salivating for that new gaming system."

"Every kid in the country is," he said on a snort. "It's the hot toy this year."

"I know. When we were in the ladies' room, your sister admitted to me that she hasn't been able to find one anywhere. All the stores she's tried have been sold out and they can't guarantee they'll get another shipment in before Christmas. She was thinking of going online and paying a private seller whatever price it takes. I talked her out of it. I told her I was pretty sure you'd already gotten them one. You should have seen the look of relief on her face."

"Great. But how are you going to track one down if she's been unsuccessful?" he asked.

She sent him a wink. "I have my ways."

He meant it when he said, "If you pull this off, they'll be in heaven."

"Yes, and you'll be their hero, Uncle Dawson."

She grinned at him and he glanced away, uncomfortable to be cast in that role. "I'll just be happy to redeem myself for the chemistry set fiasco."

"Did you pick out that gift yourself?" she asked.

"No. Carole was out of town, so I had Mrs. Stern shop for me."

"Ah, that explains it," she murmured.

"Explains what?"

"Nothing." She waved a hand and then went on. "During dessert I heard Lisa say something to your mother about a Misty Stark dress she bought recently. I was thinking that a handbag from the designer's new collection might be a winner."

"She likes handbags," he said. "She probably needs a walk-in closet just to accommodate the ones she has now."

Eve smiled at him. "I knew I liked her."

He folded his arms. "What is it with women and purses? How many do you need?"

"One to go with every outfit and to suit every mood. In other words, you can never have too many. Handbags are like shoes that way."

"You sound like my wife." The words were out and, judging from Eve's stunned expression, he wasn't going to be able to pretend he hadn't said them.

Nor was he going to be able to change the subject, he realized, when she said, "Do you mean ex-wife?"

"No. My late wife. She... she and my daughter died in a car accident." He swallowed the bitter memories and absently rubbed a hand over the scar that was partially hidden in his hairline.

"Dawson, I'm so sorry. I had no idea."

She rested a hand on his forearm and gave it a squeeze. He nodded stiffly to accept her condolences and then shifted slightly in his seat, forcing her hand to drop.

"When did this happen?"

"Three years ago." He cleared his throat. "Look, no offense, but this isn't something I care to talk about. Mind if we change the subject?"

She nodded. "Of course."

Even so, the remainder of the drive to her apartment was accomplished in silence.

Well, Eve thought, *some things about the man, not to mention the interesting reactions he'd received from family and acquaintances all evening, finally made sense.*

But far from alleviating her curiosity, this new bit of information only stoked it more.

Three years was a long time, except when tragedy was involved. Tragedies changed people. Eve knew that firsthand. As young as she'd been at the time of her mother's death, it had shaped her life. In a way, she'd lost both of parents that day—her mother to a drug overdose, her musician father to the road.

How had tragedy changed Dawson? What had the man been like before the accident? She was pretty sure she had caught glimpses of that man this evening, especially when they were around his family. She wished she could have met *that* Dawson.

When they arrived at her building, he insisted on walking her to her apartment door. Eve had expected that, so she hadn't bothered to protest. He was a gentleman, and having met his mother, Eve knew good manners had been drilled into him from an early age.

"I thought tonight was very productive," she told him as they stood on opposite sides of the small elevator.

"Good. That was the purpose."

"Yes. But I had a nice time anyway. Did you?"

His gaze was penetrating, but his words were aloof. "As you said, it was a productive evening."

"Stop," she teased. "You'll give me a big head." When he continued to stare at her, she added more seriously, "You have a wonderful family. It's obvious how much they love you."

His head jerked down in what resembled a nod.

She'd touched another nerve, she supposed, since his more immediate family was gone. Maybe she should just shut up.

The elevator dinged and bumped to a halt when it arrived at her floor. Then the doors rattled open only far enough for a person to slip through.

Dawson shot her a concerned look as she turned sideways and then had to step up six inches to reach the hallway floor. He had a harder time getting out.

"This thing is a death trap," he muttered.

"Yeah, I've called the super on it half a dozen times and I'm sure I'm not the only one in the building who has," she said as they made their way to her door. "You may want to take the stairs down," she advised.

He nodded.

Eve pulled the keys from her small clutch. She wasn't sure what prompted the invitation, but she heard herself ask, "Would you like to come in for a drink?"

She watched his jaw clench and when he spoke his words were clipped. "It's getting late."

"Right." Because she felt foolish, she teased, "Worried that you'll turn into a pumpkin?"

He snorted. "Worried that my driver might."

"Jonas, right?" She'd forgotten about him.

"Right."

"Well, I'd offer to invite Jonas in for a nightcap as

well, but I wouldn't want to give you the wrong impression about me."

Dawson's laughter was both begrudging and a surprise. "Since the first moment I met you, Eve, I've formed all sorts of impressions. I don't think I've figured you out yet." He sobered then and leaned against the door jamb, studying her in the hallway's dim lighting. "You have a lot of layers."

"If you compare me to an onion, you'll ruin what is otherwise a fairly interesting compliment."

"Why do I get the feeling you like to keep me guessing?"

She batted her lashes, going for comical when she replied, "Maybe because mystery is half my allure."

He straightened and she thought he might turn to leave. In fact, she swore he started to, but then he was closing the space between them.

In that brief moment as his mouth hovered just above hers, Dawson whispered, "Don't sell yourself short."

As kisses went this one shouldn't have rocked Eve's world. It was brief, close-mouthed and bordered on perfunctory. Yet her knees felt weak afterward.

She credited Dawson's expression for that. She'd seen the man nearly naked, but at the moment he was far more exposed. Emotions played over his face in rapid succession, so many that she could barely keep track of them all. But a couple stood out. He was angry, although not necessarily with her, and he most certainly was turned on.

We're even, she thought, as he stalked away and she closed the door. She was turned on, too.

CHAPTER SIX

"You might have mentioned something to me about Dawson's having lost his wife and child," Eve said.

She was at Carole's comfortable home just outside Denver, making good on the movie, wine, and Chinese food night that she'd previously had to cancel. Carole's leg was propped up on a pillow on the couch and an old Cary Grant movie was playing on the television, although neither one of them was watching it.

Between bites of sweet and sour pork Carole admitted, "I thought about it. In fact, I nearly did when you said he wanted you to come to the charity ball. But I wanted you to form your own impression of the man without being prejudiced by his tragic history."

"Why?"

Carole shook her head. "We'll get to that in a

minute. First, I want to hear what you think about him, especially after spending an entire evening in his company."

"You make it sound like it was a date," Eve said dryly. "It was work."

But then her gaze slid away. Well, it had been *mostly* work. The big exception of course was the kiss he'd given her at her apartment door. While it had ended well before turning into anything remotely passionate, it had been on her mind ever since. Were Dawson a different sort of man, Eve might have thought that was his intent.

Keep her guessing...

Keep her wanting...

And he said *she* had a lot of layers.

But, as it was, she doubted he'd meant to kiss her in the first place. Afterward, he'd barely managed to bid her a curt good night before stalking away.

"Are you telling me that you *didn't* enjoy yourself?" Carole asked.

"No. I enjoyed myself." It was easier to concentrate on the event rather than the man, so she added, "It was a first-rate affair. You wouldn't believe the food that was served, or the dishes the food was served on, for that matter. It was like being at a five-star restaurant. And the dessert? Sin on a plate."

"Chocolate?" Carole asked.

"Devil's food cake, red velvet cake and an assortment of tarts."

Carole made a humming sound, but then she went right back to the subject at hand. "Okay, so tell me what you thought of the man."

Eve poked through the white takeout carton with a pair of chopsticks, coming out with a piece of pickled carrot. "Let's see. He can be incredibly overbearing and arrogant. Oh, and he definitely needs to be in control all of the time," she added as she recalled their dance and the jolt it had given him when she'd taken the lead.

She still wasn't sure why she'd done that. She only knew that for some reason she'd felt the need to push him outside the rigid confines of his comfort zone.

"Anything else?" Carole's smile turned knowing. "What did you think of him physically?"

Eve heaved a dramatic sigh. "You already know that he's seriously gorgeous and just about as sexy as they come. I'd have to be dead not to find him attractive."

Carole laughed. "That was what I thought, too. Of course, when I first met him, his wife was still alive, and I had just gone through a very messy divorce. In fact, landing the Burke Financial account helped pay for my lawyer fees among other things," she said wryly. "Officially, Clive hired me and I only shopped for the business side of things. But after he retired, I worked with Dawson. And, well, after the accident, he asked me to do all the shopping—personal and professional."

"Did he give you much input? Before meeting his family at the ball, I felt like I was flying blind with their gifts."

"We spoke a few times, but mostly Rachel Stern acted as a go-between."

"Mrs. Stern," Eve muttered. "That woman needs a hobby."

But Carole waved a hand. "She's really not that bad. She's just very protective of Dawson, almost like a second mother," she said. "And speaking of mothers, what did you think of Tallulah and the rest of his family?"

Eve grinned then. "I liked them. All of them. Very much. They're nice people. Normal. Not at all hoity-toity, if you know what I mean."

"I know."

"Dawson is different around them. He's less... stuffy. They obviously love him. That much came through loud and clear."

"The Burkes are a close bunch," Carole agreed.

"Eve frowned. "Yes, but he won't shop for them. And he told a friend that he'll be heading out of town at the end of the month to spend the holidays in Cabo San Lucas. From the various comments I overheard, I couldn't help but feel he's avoiding them."

"He's avoiding life and has been since the accident," her friend replied. "As I said, it wasn't until the accident that he added his personal shopping needs to my duties."

"It sounds like he's really changed," Eve said thoughtfully.

"Oh, he has." Carole nodded. "Do you feel sorry for him, Eve?"

"Well, of course, I do. How can I not? The man lost his wife and daughter."

"Yes. In a car accident on Christmas Eve three years ago." Carole's expression turned grim. "Dawson was the one driving at the time."

"And he was the only one to survive," Eve finished. She closed her eyes. "I can only imagine how horrible that must have been."

"Yes, especially since his private hell was offered up for public consumption."

"What do you mean?"

"The Burkes are highly regarded in the community, not just because of the business, but because of their overall involvement. In addition to the charity ball, they've got their finger in just about every philanthropic venture that comes along. Dawson's late wife's family is well-known, too, so the accident received plenty of media coverage, especially since Sheila's mother had some pretty nasty things to say about him when she spoke to reporters. There was even some ugly speculation early on about drunken driving before police revealed that his blood alcohol level had been well below the legal limit."

"How awful," Eve said.

"Yes. He also was cleared of any negligence. He was driving within the speed limit at the time and, with the exception of that patch of black ice, road conditions were fine."

"In other words, it was an accident."

"Yes. An accident. And it could have happened to anyone. Still, from what I've seen and from what those who know him well say, Dawson blames himself," Carole said.

Of course, he would. He was that type of man. Duty, responsibility, family—he took such things very seriously. They were his foundation and in one fell swoop that foundation had been reduced to rubble.

"I really wish you had given me a heads up, Carole. I'm the first to admit I can be too blunt at times. I might have been a little more diplomatic, a little more sensitive if I'd understood why he needed a personal shopper to purchase gifts for his family."

"Actually, that's one of the reasons I didn't tell you," Carole surprised her by saying. "I won't presume to know Dawson well. He's more of a give-orders sort of man than the sit-down-and-chat kind. But I've always liked him and respected him. And from what I've seen since the accident, he doesn't want coddling or pity. In fact, I'd say those are the last things he wants or, frankly, needs."

"What does he need?" Eve hadn't intended to ask that question. What business was it of hers?

But when Eve glanced over at Carole, the woman's smile bordered on calculating. "I'm not sure, but maybe someone as resourceful as you are will be able to figure it out."

———

It was half past midnight and even though Dawson had gone to bed nearly two hours earlier, he was wide awake. There was nothing new about his insomnia. Since the accident he'd had a hard time falling asleep and an even harder time staying asleep once he had. The only time he actually slumbered straight through until morning was when he relied on prescription medication. But he didn't like taking the pills his doctor had prescribed. They left him feeling too fuzzy-headed the next day. So, instead, he often used the wee hours of the morning to make lists of things he needed to do and to catch up on his reading. Sadly, not even the boring article he was scanning in a business journal was making him heavy-lidded this night.

He set the magazine aside on an oath, switched off the bedside lamp and rolled over. After giving his pillow a couple of good punches to reshape it, he admitted that the sleeplessness from which he had suffered the past several nights was different.

He blamed Eve for that.

He also blamed himself.

"I never should have kissed her," he muttered into the darkness.

Why that mere peck should haunt him, he wasn't sure. At the end of the two dates he'd gone on, he had kissed both women and with far more intimacy than he had Eve. Yet neither encounter had left him wanting. Quite the opposite. Both had made him feel cold. And he had wondered if maybe even his libido had suffered irreparable damage in the accident.

Lying in the dark now, he recalled the way Eve's eyes had gone wide with surprise as he breached her personal space and settled his mouth over hers. Her lips had been soft, inviting and sorely tempting, which was why Dawson had ended things quickly. Despite that brief contact, however, there was no denying that Dawson had felt something he hadn't in a very long time: alive.

The guilt came instantly, scoring his battered heart anew. But even guilt couldn't stamp out the attraction he felt for Eve.

On a groan, he rolled over, determined to remove the woman from his mind. "I never should have kissed her," he mumbled again into his pillow.

Yet when he finally drifted off an hour later, he dreamed of doing it again and properly this time.

Eve was preparing to leave for the day when a courier knocked at her door with an official-looking envelope from Burke Financial. She tipped the young man who delivered it and went back inside her apartment to peel back the seal. Then she nearly fell over.

Inside was a pair of theater tickets for the same, sold-out musical that she'd bid on in the silent auction the previous Saturday night, only these were for better seats. Much better seats. As well as a backstage pass to meet the cast and crew afterward.

The note read:

Eve,

I saw a billboard for Les Misérables *on my way into work this morning and thought of you. Burke Financial keeps a box at the theater. I checked and no one was going to this Saturday's performance. It seemed a shame to let them go to waste. Enjoy yourself.*

Dawson

She dug her phone out of her purse and called him at his office immediately. Of course, she got his secretary.

"He has a meeting in half an hour and he's prepping for it," Mrs. Stern informed her. It sounded like a brush-off to Eve, even though the woman did ask to take a message.

She's like a second mother, Carole claimed. Eve decided to play on that. Mothers liked nothing better than women with good manners.

"He was kind enough to send me theater tickets. I hate to disturb him, but I only need a moment of his time to thank him properly. Do you think you might be able to put me through?" she asked.

"Tickets?" There was a note of surprise in the other woman's tone.

"Yes, for the Saturday evening performance of *Les Mis*. I bid on some tickets at the charity ball's silent auction, but I didn't get them."

"You were at the ball?" This nugget of information definitely came as a surprise.

"As his guest," Eve confirmed. But, worrying she might be overplaying her hand, she added, "Since so many of the people on his Christmas list would be in attendance, he felt it would help me do my job."

"I see."

Eve held her breath during the long pause that followed. Finally, Mrs. Stern said, "Just a moment. I'll put you through."

Eve was still congratulating herself on getting past Mrs. Stern when Dawson came on the line.

"Eve, what can I help you with?" He sounded tired, but not irritated by her interruption.

"Hi, Dawson. I know you're busy, but I just wanted to call and say thank you."

"I take it the tickets arrived."

"Yes. Just a moment ago. For once I was glad to be running a little behind schedule." As she spoke, she paced the length of her living room in front of the big windows that brought some of the city's skyline inside. "It's incredibly generous of you, Dawson."

"They weren't being used," he replied.

"Yes, as you mentioned in your note."

"It seemed a shame for them to go to waste when I knew how much you wanted to see the show."

But that he thought of her enough to see if the box seats were taken said something. What, exactly, she wasn't sure.

"Still, I'm grateful."

"You're welcome. Anything else?" His tone made it clear he was preparing to hang up.

She nibbled her lip. "Here's the thing. I find myself in a bit of a quandary."

"Why is that?" he asked.

"Well, I know what these tickets go for, so I feel a little awkward accepting something so valuable from a client." Which was partly true.

She pictured Dawson shrugging as he suggested, "Consider it a bonus."

"That's very generous of you, but my commission is all the bonus I require." Eve twisted a lock of hair around her index finger as an idea took shape. It was only half-formed when she blurted it out. "Perhaps you would consider coming with me to see the play?"

The invitation was met with deafening and prolonged silence, making her regret her haste in issuing it.

"Ok*aaaay*. Apparently not. It was just a thought. You've probably already seen the show," she said, in an attempt to save face. Not that she actually thought it was possible to save face at this point. She had essentially asked this man—her client, for all intents and purposes her boss—out. "I'll let you get back to work now. Bye." She hit the disconnect button on her phone without giving him a chance to reply.

"I am such an idiot." She muttered in mortification and shuffled back a couple steps so she could flop unceremoniously onto the couch.

What had she been thinking, offering an invitation like that? The man was probably seriously regretting his generosity right about now. She knew she was regretting her spontaneity. She slumped to one side on the sofa and stared up at the ceiling in disgust. As she laid amid the throw pillows and mentally berated herself, her cellphone trilled. Eve glanced at the caller ID and bolted upright.

"Hello?"

He didn't return the greeting. Instead, he said, "You hung up on me awfully fast. I didn't get a chance to give you an answer."

She ran a hand through the hair she had spent

half an hour taming with a blow dryer and an assortment of products. "I guess I took your silence for an answer."

"Yeah. I'm sorry about that. I was just a little... surprised," he told her.

"I got that," she replied. Indeed, it had come through loud and clear.

"When I sent the tickets, I just assumed you would have someone else in mind for the second one."

"Such as?" she prodded.

"I don't know. Maybe the date you had to cancel on the night of the charity ball," he replied.

"Oh, that." Because he couldn't see her expression, she let her grin unfurl. She doubted he was jealous, but she still liked knowing that he paid attention to the things she said. She continued. "It was nothing serious. I was just getting together with a friend."

"A friend." Dawson cleared his throat. "And would this friend be male or female?"

His reply gave her ego another little boost and gave her the courage to ask, "Does it matter?"

"No. It's none of my business."

"Female," she supplied anyway.

"Ah."

The man went infuriatingly quiet again. Too quiet. Eve began ticking off the seconds in her head as the silence drew out. When she got to fifteen, she blurted out, "You're doing it again."

"Doing what?"

"Not saying anything, which forces me to draw my own conclusions."

"And what conclusions might those be?" Amusement tinged his tone.

Pinching her eyes closed, she gave into impulse. "You're trying to figure out which restaurant you want to take me to for dinner before we head to the theater Saturday night."

While Eve held her breath, she heard a mild oath and then strangled laughter. Her lungs felt close to bursting by the time Dawson finally got around to saying, "It's like you're a mind reader."

CHAPTER SEVEN

The telephone rang as Eve reapplied her lipstick in the mirror that hung over a console table near her apartment door. Though it wasn't her style to appear eager, she was wearing her coat and had been trying not to watch the clock.

"Eve, it's Dawson. I'm really sorry, but I'm running a little behind," he told her unnecessarily. She had expected him to arrive twenty minutes earlier. Their dinner reservation at Tulane, a swanky new restaurant that Eve was dying to try, was for six o'clock and that time was fast approaching.

"Is everything... okay?" she inquired.

"Wondering if I've changed my mind?"

No... Yes... She settled on, "I would understand."

And as disappointed as she would be, she *would* understand, given everything she now knew about his past.

While Eve wasn't considering tonight to be a full-fledged date, neither would her conscience allow her to classify it as mere business. She found Dawson interesting, handsome, and definitely sexy. Generally speaking, she made it a rule not to become romantically involved with her male clients. But since the Burke account was hers only temporarily courtesy of Carole, she felt safe making an exception.

"I'm not going to stand you up, Eve." His tone was resolute. "It's just that something came up at the last minute."

"Okay. How about I meet you at Tulane then?" she suggested. The restaurant wasn't far from her apartment and it would save him from having to backtrack, as the place was located between them.

He hesitated and Eve was reminded of the fact that he preferred to take the lead. But then he said, "All right. I'll call and let them know we are running late and not to give away our reservation. But give me another fifteen minutes before you leave."

"Got it."

"And, if I'm not there when you arrive, order an appetizer," he added. "And a glass of wine, if you'd like."

"Should I start dinner without you, too?" she asked dryly.

"No." He chuckled. "I'll be there."

Eve had barely been at the restaurant fifteen minutes when Dawson walked through the doors at

Tulane. He had shed his overcoat at the coat check. Beneath it he wore a tailored charcoal suit, white dress shirt, and muted print tie. He looked sophisticated, sexy, and just a tad arrogant as he scanned the tables. When he spotted her, he didn't smile exactly, but his intense expression relaxed even as it brightened, and he nodded in her direction. Eve sucked in a breath and exhaled it slowly between her teeth, trying to appear unaffected as he made his way to their table. He reached it just as the waiter was bringing the artichoke dip she had ordered.

"Sorry I'm late," he apologized again as he slipped onto the chair opposite hers.

Her heart rate once again normal, she offered him an easy smile. "That's okay. I haven't been here very long."

The server cleared his throat. "I'll be back in a few minutes to take your order."

"Very good," Dawson told the young man. To Eve, he said, "I see you got us an appetizer."

"Yes. I hope you like artichoke dip and toast squares," she said.

"You won't hear me complaining." He shook out his napkin and laid it over his lap. "I'm famished."

"I also took a chance and had the waiter bring us a bottle of wine."

He picked it up and scanned the label. His brow beetled as his gaze connected with hers. "Pinot noir. And this is my favorite vintage. How did you know?"

"It's what you were drinking the other night."

"You certainly pay attention." He poured them both a glass.

Eve picked hers up and shrugged. "I tend to remember details."

Over the rim of his glass, Dawson studied Eve. He remembered details, too. When it came to Eve Hawley, he recalled far too many of them for his own peace of mind.

Details such as the golden flecks that could be teased from her otherwise brown eyes. The candlelight was accomplishing that right now. And the paleness of her skin that contrasted with a trio of beauty marks at the base of her throat.

She was wearing black tonight. The dress's cut was simple, elegant, and even though it sported three-quarter-length sleeves and a rather demure neckline, it was every bit as sexy as the siren red number she'd had on the other evening. As for her hair, she'd left it down. It hung in a glossy dark cloud around her shoulders. Dawson wondered if it would feel as soft as it looked. If it would smell...

"You're staring at me and not saying anything." Eve's words snapped him out of his stupor. Her full lips bowed when she added, "I'd wonder if I had a piece of artichoke stuck in my front teeth, but I haven't tried the dip yet."

Ah, yes, Dawson thought, and then there was that—the woman's surprisingly direct nature. It was another detail, another characteristic, that made her stand out in a crowd. His late wife had been much more reserved and...

He sipped his wine to wash away the memory before it could fully form. No, he wouldn't think of Sheila tonight. He'd done that on his other dates, he realized now, spending the time making comparisons, and finding his companions lacking. Both women had been smart, attractive, and nice, but it struck Dawson now how much they had been like his late wife, resembling Sheila in both looks and temperament. Had he unconsciously been seeking a substitute?

Eve was no stand-in. She and Sheila were polar opposites in everything from their personality to their physical characteristics. In fact, he couldn't recall ever being attracted to a woman who was quite so outspoken, independent, and vivacious. Making comparisons wouldn't be fair to either woman. Besides, what purpose would they serve? Beyond making Dawson feel guilty.

He took another sip of his wine and swore he felt a couple shackles from the past fall away when he said, "I'm staring because you look amazing this evening."

"Oh." She smiled and, in the restaurant's low light, he thought he saw her cheeks flush. The reaction seemed out of character, as did her whispered, "Thank you."

"Actually, I should thank you. I'm glad you asked me to accompany you to the theater tonight."

Her brows rose at that. "Really?"

He set his glass of wine aside. "Yes. I haven't been to the theater in ages."

Her expression turned incredulous. "Do you mean to tell me that your company has access to a pair of choice seats and you don't bother to go?"

"I've been—"

"Busy," she supplied for him, but her challenging expression told Dawson exactly what she thought of his long-standing excuse.

"I have been busy," he insisted. When his conscience delivered a sharp kick, he admitted, "All right, the truth is I don't go out much these days."

"No, the truth is you don't make *time* to go out much these days," she told him.

Direct. Definitely direct, he thought.

"They're sort of the same thing."

He thought she might argue, but she let it go and smiled instead. "I suppose I should feel flattered then that you accepted my invitation."

"Well, you're a hard woman to turn down, Eve Hawley."

He meant it. He'd spent the past few days wondering why he'd agreed to go. Even amid his many doubts and regrets, however, he hadn't considered cancelling on her. He had actually been looking forward to it.

Her smile widened. "I like that answer."

He laughed, the last of the tension leaving his shoulders. "I thought you might."

The waiter returned a moment later to tell them about the evening's dinner specials and take their orders. Eve gave the young man her undivided attention, nodding and making appreciative noises as he described the pressed duck.

"Ooh. It sounds wonderful, Danny," she said, flashing a smile that was warm rather than flirtatious.

The woman had a way with people, Dawson thought. It was more than the fact that she treated them with respect. Eve made them feel singled out, special. She didn't just acknowledge people, she connected with them.

After they'd placed their orders and the waiter was gone, Dawson said, "You know, you're very good at that."

"At what?"

"At making people feel like they're important," he replied.

Her brows rose at the same time her chin dipped down and she pinned him with a stare that would have done the headmistress of prep school proud. "That's because people *are* important."

"You know what I mean."

"No, I don't. And I'm going to be very disappointed if you suddenly turn into a snob," she informed him. Even though she said it lightly, he didn't doubt that she meant it.

"I am not a snob." When she remained silent, he raised one hand palm up as if taking an oath. "On my honor, Eve, I swear that I am not a snob. My mother wouldn't allow it."

Eve's expression softened then. "Since I have met your mother, not to mention the rest of your lovely family, I believe you."

"That's a relief," he teased before growing serious. "For the record, my observation just now was intended to be a compliment. A lot of people wouldn't bother to make eye contact with a waiter, much less call him by his given name."

"Oh, Danny and I go way back."

"You know him?" Dawson blinked in surprise.

But Eve grinned and leaned forward, as if imparting a secret when she said in a low voice, "We met when I ordered the appetizer."

"You just—what?—introduced yourself?"

She started to laugh. "I didn't have to. His name is on the badge that's pinned to his shirt." Her expression turned thoughtful. "Maybe we all should be wearing name tags. It would make things more personal."

"That it would." As idealistic and unrealistic as he found her comment, he couldn't bring himself to disagree.

"Besides, how should I refer to him? 'Hey, you?'

Or maybe I should just snap my fingers to gain his attention? I really hate finger-snappers," she muttered.

He agreed with her on that point.

"I know some people who snap their fingers in restaurants."

She shook her head and looked disappointed. "You need to start hanging around with a better class of friends."

"I didn't say they were my friends. I just said I knew such people. They think they're better than everyone else because their bank accounts are large."

"The ones who are born into money are the worst," she replied, adding hastily, "Present company excluded, of course."

"Of course."

She twirled her wine glass by its stem before taking a sip. Then she surprised him by saying, "I was in a relationship with one of those people for a couple of years, although it took me a while to figure out that he was just slumming."

A couple of years? "It sounds like the two of you were pretty serious."

"I thought so at the time." She selected a piece of toast and scooped up some of the artichoke dip. Before popping it into her mouth, she added, "It turned out that while I was good enough to spend time with, neither he nor his parents felt I had the right pedigree to carry on the family bloodline, or some such nonsense."

The evening of the ball, Dawson had sensed vulnerability. Despite her cavalier attitude now, it made an appearance again, and he thought he understood the reason for it.

"I'm sorry," he said.

She waved away his apology.

"Drew did offer to keep seeing me provided that we met on the down-low. He said that he had a lot of fun whenever we were together and he hated for that to end."

I bet, Dawson thought.

"Good for you that you turned him down."

"Well, he made it pretty easy. He'd already announced his engagement to a woman who it turned out he'd been dating on and off since grad school. Hence the need for our discretion." She made a tsking sound and in a rueful voice asked, "Why is it that the other woman is always the last to know?"

"Sorry," he said again. "Does this Drew character live around here? Maybe I could go to his house and beat him up for you."

It was said in jest, but afterward Dawson realized he actually wouldn't mind paying the other man a visit.

Eve tilted her head to one side and studied him. "Hmm. I appreciate the offer and all, but I don't know. You don't strike me as a brawler."

"It's not my usual style," he agreed.

"Let me guess. You prefer diplomacy."

"Diplomacy has its place." He nodded thoughtfully before taking a sip of his wine. "But so does a carefully landed punch."

She laughed. "Well, as tempting as I find your offer, I'm afraid Drew is back in Connecticut, no doubt making the rounds in polite society with his new bride."

"Connecticut?" Dawson frowned. "I thought you said you were from Maine?"

"I said I was born in Maine," she replied. "But I moved to Connecticut when I was eight and then a few other states along the Eastern Seaboard. I ended up in Hartford after college."

"It sounds like you moved around a lot."

"I did."

She selected another piece of toast, and something told him that no more information on her childhood would be forthcoming. Oddly, he was disappointed. He'd been bored to tears when his other two dates had gone on about their personal lives. But Eve was an intriguing puzzle, and he wanted to discover more of the missing pieces.

"So, I'd have to travel to Connecticut if I wanted to beat up your ex?" he teased.

"Nah. He's not worth the price of the airfare. Besides, I'm over it."

Over it? Dawson thought as he helped himself to

the appetizer. Perhaps Eve was over the man—and he chose not to examine too closely why he hoped that was the case—but she was not over the slight. No, that wound had definitely not healed yet.

"Well, if it's any consolation, it doesn't sound like his marriage will last very long, let alone be a very happy one," Dawson told her.

"No. Probably not." She dabbed her mouth with her napkin, pulling it away to reveal a devilish smile. "I know it's incredibly small of me, but I hope she takes him to the cleaners when they divorce."

"It would serve him right," Dawson agreed. "In my opinion, a man who can't be faithful to a woman deserves to lose something even more, um, personal than money."

Eve grinned at him. "I knew there was a reason I liked you. Well, besides your penchant for a good bubble bath."

"That was for charity," he reminded her with an exaggerated sigh, but then he couldn't help grinning back.

He liked Eve, too. She not only made it easy to carry on a conversation, she made it easy to joke. He'd almost forgotten that he possessed a sense of humor. It resurfaced now as he asked, "Do you mean my wit and charm weren't enough reasons?"

"Witty and charming are not the two adjectives I would have used to describe you when we first met.

Even if I did appreciate the view." Her eyebrows bobbed comically.

Dawson grimaced as he recalled that meeting at his house and his state of undress. "Is it too late to apologize for that?"

"As far as I'm concerned, it's never too late to apologize for anything," she replied.

"How very magnanimous of you. In that case, I am sorry." He decided to come clean. "The truth is I wasn't in the best mood that day. I was hoping to get rid of you quickly."

"Do tell." She picked up her wine and sipped. "And—what?—you thought I'd run screaming in the opposite direction at the sight of a naked man?"

Unfortunately, the waiter picked that exact moment to arrive with their dinner salads. The young man cleared his throat and glanced from Dawson to Eve as he set the plates on the table.

"It wasn't as scandalous as it sounds," she assured the waiter. Sending a wink to Dawson, she added, "It was a business meeting, but he wasn't expecting me, which is why he was naked."

It took an effort for Dawson not to squirm in his seat. It wasn't that Eve didn't have a filter. Rather, he got the feeling she enjoyed not employing it on occasion, just to keep him off-balance. And he certainly was off-balance.

The young man wisely chose to ignore Eve's clarification and cleared his throat again. "Would you care for freshly ground pepper on your salad, miss?"

He held out the wooden mill.

"Please," Eve replied, looking not the least bit embarrassed. Dawson, on the other hand, was pretty sure his face was still the same color as the raspberry vinaigrette dressing that was drizzled over his plate of baby mixed greens.

"And you, sir?"

"No, thank you."

"Very good. Your main courses will be up shortly. Can I get either of you anything else before then?" the young man inquired politely.

"No, Danny." She glanced across the table at Dawson and winked. "I think we're... covered."

When they were alone again, Dawson said, "Just as a point of clarification, I was not naked when we met."

"Oh, that's right. You were wearing a sheet." But Eve caused him to blush all over again when she added, "I guess I must have let my imagination fill in all the parts that sheet concealed."

On a strangled laugh, Dawson replied, "I hope your imagination did me justice."

"Oh, I don't think you need to be concerned on that score."

A potent silence stretched between them before Dawson replied quietly, "I guess we'll see."

His response and what it implied had Eve's

mouth dropping open a moment before she closed it and her lips curved. But they both seemed well aware that they were treading close to a line neither of them was quite ready to cross. Certainly, Dawson wasn't. So, it came as a relief that by the time Danny returned with their entrees, their conversation had veered to far safer topics of conversation than Dawson's anatomy.

An hour later, they had finished their meal and paid the tab, which Eve insisted on picking up. She was a little surprised when Dawson didn't object. He had opened his mouth as if to protest, but then he merely said, "I'll leave the tip."

As they were leaving the restaurant Eve spied his limousine waiting at the curb just up the street. She turned to him and said, "You know, my Tahoe is in the parking garage. Why don't you give your driver the rest of the night off? I can get us to the theater." She sent him an angelic smile and added, "Afterward, I promise to be a perfect gentleman and drop you off at your home well before you turn into a pumpkin."

Dawson glanced at the limo where his omnipresent driver had already hopped out and was waiting to open the rear door. Eve braced for his protest, but once again he surprised her by agreeing.

"All right. I guess that makes more sense than taking separate vehicles to the theater."

He excused himself to dismiss his driver and then they walked to the parking garage across the street. Even more surprising than his agreement to take her vehicle was the fact that Dawson didn't insist on getting behind the wheel when they reached the Tahoe. Without a word, he got in on the passenger's side–after opening the driver's door for her, of course. If she saw his mother again, Eve would be sure to compliment Tallulah on her son's excellent manners.

"I'm not sure I've ever met a man who was willing to relinquish the driver's seat, especially to a woman," she joked after starting the vehicle.

She glanced over at Dawson in the Tahoe's dim interior as he started the engine. Far from smiling, his face was drawn, his lips compressed into a tight line. Something was wrong.

He was a man who preferred to be in control at all times, yet not only was he willing to let her drive, it occurred to Eve that he paid someone else to do the driving for him on a regular basis. Before, Eve had considered that the prerogative of a wealthy businessman. He could afford such a luxury and so he used it and enjoyed it. It struck her now, however, that, as the lone survivor of a harrowing crash, hiring a driver had really been more of a necessity.

Dawson Burke-powerful, intelligent, and pragmatic man though he was—was afraid to drive.

To fill the awkward silence, Eve said, "Um, just to put your mind at ease, I've never had so much as a parking ticket."

"Good to know," came his clipped response.

Out of the corner of her eye, she watched him buckle his seat belt and then pull on the strap as if testing it. Afterward, he rested the palms of his hand on his thighs, hardly the picture of relaxation. In the rear of a limo, it was probably easy to forget about oncoming traffic, but that wasn't the case with a front-seat view.

"It's nice to be able to leave the driving to other people, isn't it?" she said, not so much in an effort to make small talk as to let him know that she understood his reticence.

Dawson responded with a tight-lipped, "Yes," as she backed out of the parking space and then shifted into drive.

"You probably get a lot of work done on your morning commute."

"Yes." Another laconic reply.

She followed the signs to the exit and paid the fee to the attendant. As the gate's arm rose, she told Dawson, "I'd love to be able to spend my commute reading or what not. I try to time it so I'm not on the roads at the height of rush hour. Traffic can be a killer, especially on the area highways." As soon as the words were out, she wanted to snatch them back. If Eve hadn't needed to keep her foot on the gas pedal, she would have used it to kick herself. Talk about a poor choice of words.

Dawson, however, answered with an honest, "Yes. The highways can be a real killer."

"Gosh, Dawson. I'm sorry. That came out wrong."

"No need to apologize, but you'd better pull forward before the gate comes down again."

They reached the street and she turned the Tahoe right and merged into traffic.

"You told me before that you don't like to talk about the accident." She refrained from adding that he probably should, rather than keeping all of his grief and self-blame bottled up inside. Her thoughts turned to her father, a perpetual man-child whose grief had left him emotionally stunted. It wasn't healthy, Eve knew firsthand.

"We weren't talking about the accident," he said. "And we're not."

"But Dawson—"

"We're talking about driving. I prefer to leave that job to other people, so I hired a driver."

She allowed him the out, even though they both knew he was lying.

"Ah. Right. Well, I live for the day that I will not only be able to afford to hire a driver but pay someone to clean my toilets. Now, that's a chore I would be happy to pawn off on someone else. It's nasty."

"I'll have to take your word for it," he replied blandly.

"Do you mean to tell me you've never scrubbed a commode?" she asked. "Not even when you were a kid?"

"No."

"Didn't your parents make you do chores?" Tallulah and Clive seemed so down-to-earth despite their wealth that Eve assumed he had.

"Sure, we did chores. Just not cleaning toilets or scrubbing floors or that kind of thing. We had a housekeeper."

"What other kinds of chores are there?"

"We helped with my mother's charity events. And before you say that doesn't count, I'll remind you that my mother can be incredibly detail-oriented and particular when it comes to her events."

"Well, I clean my toilet every Saturday morning if you ever feel the need to rack up another life experience," she offered.

As she turned onto Curtis Street, she glanced over in time to see his lips loosen with the beginnings of a smile.

"I'll keep that in mind," he said.

CHAPTER EIGHT

"So, was the performance as good as you hoped?" he asked as they left the theater and headed to her Tahoe. It was parked only a couple blocks away, but the wind had turned the night from crisp to downright bitter.

"It was even better and the seats were amazing," she said. Her words were slightly muffled by the scarf that was wound around her neck. "I still can't believe I got to meet the cast and crew."

Eve had seemed to enjoy herself when they were allowed backstage, although Dawson had been a little surprised by how tongue-tied she'd been.

At one point, he had leaned over to whisper in her ear, "They're just people. Same as you."

But she'd shook her head and whispered back, "They're incredibly talented people."

He liked this fangirl side of her, since she seemed

to take almost everything else in stride. Eventually, she loosened up enough to enjoy a glass of Pellegrino and some cheese from what she referred to as "the mother of all charcuterie boards."

He had to admit, the arrangement of meats and cheeses, fruit and assorted olives and nuts, was rather lavish. If both of them hadn't still been full from their meal at Tulane, they might have sampled more.

Now, as she fished the key fob out of her handbag while they walked, she was humming one of the musical's more upbeat tunes.

"That song is going to be stuck in my head for days," he complained, but he was only teasing. And he wasn't being totally honest, because it wasn't the song that would be in his head. It was this woman. It was the way she had looked tonight. The way she looked right now. She radiated happiness, excitement and contentment, all of which made her appear even more breath-taking.

"I know," Eve was saying. "But I don't mind. I love it." She stopped walking and turned sideways, taking his hand in her gloved one and giving it a companionable squeeze. "Thank you again for coming with me."

"You're welcome."

They started to walk again. He wondered if she realized she was still holding his hand. That innocuous contact was doing funny things to his heart rate.

"So, did you enjoy it?" she asked.

"What?"

She started to laugh. "The play. What else?"

Dawson cleared his throat and attempted to clear his head.

"Sure. Of course." Then he confessed, "You know, this wasn't my first time seeing *Les Mis.*"

"Get out!" A puff of white mist accompanied her exclamation and even though she was holding his hand, she stepped closer and bumped his shoulder with hers as they walked.

"This was actually the third time," he admitted.

"Here I thought you were a virgin, and it turns out you have some experience," she replied wryly.

He laughed at her phrasing, and tried to ignore the way both it and the sideways smile she sent him further stoked the attraction building inside him.

Keeping his tone light, he replied, "The first time was many years ago when it was still on Broadway. I was just a kid. My parents took my sister and me to New York for a weekend and surprised us with a matinee performance."

"You're so lucky. I bet you had awesome seats."

"We did. Fifth row, center." When she sighed, he added, "But we didn't get to meet the cast afterward."

"Still, you must have loved it. I mean, you went and saw it again. How old were you then?"

"Just out of college. My grandfather asked me to take a client."

"Did you find it even better the second time? You know, because you were an adult and understood the story?"

He debated with himself a moment before admitting, "I fell asleep right after Fantine's death scene."

"You did not!" She sounded scandalized.

"In my defense, I had stayed up late the night before and—"

She cut him off. "Sorry, Dawson, there's no defense for that."

"Well, I enjoyed myself tonight."

And he had. He credited Eve for that. Her excitement and engagement throughout the performance had been contagious. She had laughed out loud and clapped at the ribald antics of the Thénardiers, and then cried when Jean Valjean made his passionate plea to God to spare Marius's life. At times, he'd found himself more interested in watching her than the actors performing on the stage.

Just as he enjoyed watching her now. They had reached her Tahoe and were settled inside. She unwound her scarf, revealing the slender line of her neck, which her upswept hair exposed.

"Do you like the music at least?" she asked, pulling him from his introspection.

"I... I do." Especially when she was humming it slightly off key like she was now as she adjusted the heat vent and then pulled on her seatbelt.

"You can download it online, or I actually still

have it on CD." She smiled over at him as she pointed to the CD player in the dashboard. It was an older model Tahoe. Newer vehicles no longer offered that outdated option. "I have the disc in my console. I could dig it out and we could listen to it on the ride home if you'd like."

"Thanks, but I'll pass. Don't get me wrong. The music is outstanding," he was quick to add when she looked disappointed. "It's just that show tunes aren't really my style."

Eve seemed to consider that for a moment, and then she asked, "So, what *is* your style?"

"I'm more of a vintage rock fan," he admitted. It wasn't something many people outside his family knew about him. "You know, pounding bass and wicked guitar riffs."

"Get out."

They had just pulled into traffic but had to stop almost immediately for a red light, which was a good thing as she turned in her seat to gape at him. Oddly, he wasn't feeling as tense as he had on the drive to the theater.

"I'm serious. I like music with a beat that gets the blood pumping."

Eve smiled at him, and he swallowed hard as the phrase took on a new meaning.

"Blood pumping, right." She nodded as if in agreement, but shattered the illusion by adding, "Don't forget men with seriously bad hair styles wearing spandex and screaming out indecipherable lyrics at the tops of their lungs."

She had a point about the bad hair and spandex. He fiddled with his gloves and muttered, "I can figure out the lyrics."

When she merely tipped down her chin and arched her brows, he amended, "Well, most of the time."

The light changed and she pulled forward. As she switched lanes so she could turn at the next light, she mused, "When I was a little girl, I dreamed about a career on Broadway. My goal was to be cast as Belle in the stage production of *Beauty and the Beast*. I had all the songs memorized, and I rehearsed them daily in front of the bathroom mirror."

"So, you have a good singing voice?" he asked, even though he figured he already knew the answer given her off-key humming.

She shook her head. "I couldn't carry a tune even if it came with handles, which pretty much killed Broadway as a career choice."

Dawson laughed. "I suppose that would nip things in the bud. How old were you at the time?"

"Eleven. My dad told me I should keep at it, even though it was obvious I had no talent. He's a musician. I guess I didn't get those genes."

It was one of the few references Eve had ever made to her family. Dawson realized he wanted to know more. "Really? What kind of musician is your father?"

Her tone took on an edge that Dawson had never heard her use before when she replied, "The wannabe kind. He plays old-school rock, leaning toward heavy metal."

"Hence your objection to the genre."

She merely shrugged.

"So, you wanted to follow in your dad's footsteps," Dawson said.

Eve snorted indelicately. "Only if they led me right to him. He was away. A lot," she added. "Actually, my goal was to become a major stage star, an unrivaled success. I wanted my name in lights, as the saying goes."

It was pretty easy for Dawson to read between the lines. "You wanted your father's attention."

"Sure I did. Sometimes I still do. There's nothing unusual about that. Every girl wants her father's attention," she stated matter-of-factly, but he noted the stiff set to her shoulders, the rigid line of her jaw.

Yes, all children wanted their parents' attention, but not all of them got it. Dawson had been lucky in that regard. He'd had it in spades. Still did, come to that. But Eve? Apparently not.

She slowed the vehicle as they approached another intersection. When she was fully stopped for the light, she pulled up his address in her contacts and plugged it into her maps app. After a disembodied voice began directing their route, she redirected the conversation.

"What did you want to be when you were growing up?"

"Do you mean before I figured out that I didn't look so good in long hair and spandex, or after I accepted the fact that the National Football League wasn't going to come recruiting?"

Her lips twitched as she drove. "Either-or. Surprise me."

He rubbed a hand over his chin, thinking. "Well, I pretty much always knew I'd go into the family business. It suited my personal interests, not to mention my academic strengths. I didn't feel pressured to do it or anything." Dawson leaned back in his seat, relaxing a little more as he recalled the advice his father had given him just before he'd gone off to college.

Do what makes you happy, son. Not what you think will make me happy.

"My dad would have understood if I had chosen a different career. My grandfather would have been livid, but Dad... No, he would have understood and been supportive."

He smiled after saying it, feeling a kind of warmth that had nothing to do with the heat that was finally spewing from the Tahoe's vents.

"The two of you seem really close," Eve noted.

"We are. Yes." He cleared his throat, a little

embarrassed to have been lost in nostalgia. Memories had been his nemesis for the past few years, proving so hurtful that he had blocked out the good along with the bad.

"I know this is none of my business," Eve began. "But I'm going to ask anyway. If the two of you are so close, then why are you estranged?"

Her question left Dawson staggered. "My dad and I aren't estranged."

Eve transferred her gaze from the road to Dawson. "If you're not estranged, then why are you spending the holidays in Cabo rather than with your family here?"

I don't have a family.

Sheila, Isabelle... They were gone and he was alone. But he knew they weren't the family to which Eve was referring. For the first time since leaving the theater in her Tahoe, he felt vulnerable, afraid. He tugged at the strap of his seat belt, pulling it tighter over his lap. "It's... complicated."

"I don't doubt that," she replied, returning her attention to the road briefly before they stopped for yet another light. "Life tends to get that way from time to time for everyone. That's especially true after a tragedy such as you experienced. But it sure seems like you're punishing them, Dawson."

"You're wrong, Eve. Way, *way* off base," he insisted.

If Dawson was punishing anyone, it wasn't his parents or his sister and her family. It was himself.

"It sure seems that way," she replied in a soft voice.

"That's because you don't understand."

Nobody did. They hadn't been trapped inside that crumpled-up car while a passel of emergency workers tried unsuccessfully to revive his wife. They hadn't been the ones pleading with firefighters to hurry as they finally managed to free his daughter from her safety restraint in the mangled back seat.

In the Tahoe's dimly lit interior Eve's expression radiated with sincerity when she invited, "Then help me understand, Dawson. Better yet, help *them* understand."

"I..." But the words remained stubbornly lodged in his throat. The only ones to finally make it free were, "The traffic light is green."

Dawson's chest tightened and the muscles in his shoulders and back tensed as she accelerated.

Eve parked the Tahoe in the circular drive in front of Dawson's home. The rest of the ride from the theater had been accomplished in strained silence. She accepted the blame for that. She shouldn't have pushed him so hard.

She wasn't sure exactly why she had, except that she had hoped by talking about the accident he would finally see it had been just that–an accident. It wasn't his fault. She wanted him to accept what everyone else knew. Dawson was as much a victim, a casualty, as his late wife and little daughter had been.

"Here we are," she said in an overly bright voice. "I know I've already thanked you for the tickets, but I want to do so again. I had a really nice time tonight, Dawson."

"You're welcome. I did, too."

"I'm glad you're still able to say that. I'm sorry about..." She made a winding motion with her right hand, opting not to plow that rocky ground a second time.

He caught her fingers and gave them a gentle squeeze. "How about we just forget that part, okay?"

Eve didn't think forgetting was possible, much less wise. As far as she could tell, trying to sweep the matter and his emotions under the rug was at the crux of Dawson's problem. But for the moment, she agreed. It made no sense to keep pushing him tonight.

She smiled. "All right."

Dawson had yet to release her hand. Even though they were both wearing gloves, she swore she could feel the heat from his fingers warming hers through two layers of lined leather.

His thumb began to rub the palm of her hand. She had never considered her palm, or any other place on her hand for that matter, to be an erogenous zone. But it turned out she was wrong.

Very, very wrong.

Eve swallowed a moan and stammered, "S-so, should I walk you to your front door? I mean, I did promise to be a gentleman and all."

"No need for that."

The palm caress continued. "Mmm-kay," she managed.

"If you walk me to my door, I'd only feel obligated to walk you back to your car afterward." One side of his mouth lifted. "I can't let you be the only gentleman."

"Well, I guess I had better stay here then. Otherwise, it sounds like we could pass the entire night walking back and forth between my Tahoe and your front porch."

"That would make for a long night."

"Very long," she agreed.

"And it's cold outside."

"Below freezing." She shivered, although the reaction had less to do with Denver's current temperature than the ministrations of his thumb.

"We'd have to move fast to stay warm," he told her. In contrast, the smile he offered was slow and seductive.

"If we jogged, I suppose it could be considered aerobic exercise."

"Exercise, hmm?" His thumb stopped moving

and Dawson released her hand. Gaze steady, expression serious, he removed his gloves, tugging them off one finger at a time. Anticipation hummed and built to a crescendo inside Eve until he reached for her across the vehicle's console. His big, warm hands framed her face and drew her toward him.

"I can think of more interesting methods of increasing my heart rate while in the company of a beautiful woman," he murmured, just before kissing her.

Soft. That was Eve's first thought. Even though so much of the man was hard and uncompromising, his lips were soft, their pressure gentle. She thought he might end things as quickly as he had the night of the ball, when he had abandoned her on her doorstep wondering and wanting. But he didn't.

"Eve." Dawson whispered her name as he changed the angle of their mouths and the kiss deepened.

His hands were in her hair now, his fingers lacing through it. Slow? Soft? Nothing about the man fit these descriptions now. Urgent was the word that came to mind as he fumbled with the fat buttons on the front of her wool coat. She shifted in her seat to improve his access. Her elbow connected with the steering wheel and the horn blasted loudly, blowing a hole right through the intimacy of the moment. Desire took a hasty back seat to reality.

Eve sucked in a breath as Dawson pulled away.

Her body was sizzling, snapping like an exposed electrical wire. Had she ever been this turned on? A glance in Dawson's direction had her swallowing the suggestive remark she'd been about to make. The timing would be wrong and the flirty comment unwelcome. He was slumped back in his seat, scrubbing his hands down his face.

Regrets.

She could see them as clearly as if they had been tattooed on his forehead. She could hear them, even though he had yet to say a word. They were there in his deep sigh. Eve closed her own eyes and mentally kicked herself. A moment ago, she had been thinking that the only thing standing between the pair of them was the vehicle's inconveniently placed console and their many layers of clothing.

But now she knew there was so much more than that.

"You're not ready for... this. Are you?"

"That's not exactly the issue at the moment."

His laughter was both brittle and bitter. She took no offense, though, because she knew it was directed more at himself than her.

"I'm not talking physically, Dawson."

"No." He swore and continued to stare straight ahead when he admitted, "I don't know."

"It's okay," she assured him, even as his uncertainty caused her own heart to ache.

"It's not okay!" He cursed again, this time with

more force and creativity. It was a moment before he turned to face her. She saw anger and frustration, neither of which was directed at her. "None of this is okay, Eve. None of it."

His clipped words echoed in the vehicle. She remained silent, waiting for him to continue. After a long moment, he did. His tone had lost its angry edge. Now Dawson just sounded tired and a little lost when he told her, "Some people can just go with the flow. Not me. I'm not wired that way. I had my life all figured out, you know? I made plans and then I followed through with them."

"You're talking about before the accident?"

"Yes. I made plans," he said a second time. A note of bewilderment had crept into his tone, contrasting with the belligerence that was already there.

Of course, he had. Dawson was the sort of man who needed to take charge, to be in control, whether in business or in his personal life. But tragedy and grief did not follow orders. On the contrary. Once they showed up, they called all the shots.

"Maybe it's time to make new plans," Eve offered softly.

He faced her now, his gaze glittering hard in the meager glow cast by the landscaping lights. "I did. After the accident I made new plans. I've been living my life according to them ever since."

She swallowed. "And?"

"You seem to be botching them up, Eve."

Her mouth gaped open, his shocking words still reverberating in her mind, when Dawson got out of the Tahoe and slammed the door behind him.

He was already in his house by the time her surprise wore off. It was several more minutes before Eve felt steady enough to drive home.

The rest of the weekend proved long, as did the following week for Dawson. He had plenty of work to keep him busy at the office, and he finalized his travel plans for his upcoming trip to Cabo San Lucas. Eve called him, both on his cell and at his office. He'd let the calls go to voicemail or, when he was at the office, he gave Mrs. Stern excuses for why he wasn't available to speak with her.

You're not ready for this, are you?

Eve's question taunted him. Did he want to be ready? Was a new relationship something he deserved?

When Friday dawned, he felt a sense of relief as he marked another week off his calendar. Just two more to go until he boarded a plane and left everything and everyone behind for a while. Maybe the time away would help Dawson get his head together. He knew from past experience it wouldn't do much to dull the ache in his heart or dampen his self-recrimination.

He got out of bed and stumbled through his morning routine, beyond grateful when his Keurig spat out a piping hot cup of his favorite dark roast. He downed half the cup and was feeling nearly human and ready to tackle the day until he pulled open the blinds and got his first glimpse of the weather. It was snowing, coming down in a white curtain that made it impossible to see much of his yard.

The forecast had called for flurries, not a damned blizzard, so the accumulation that blanketed the landscape, turning shrubs and trees into blobs of white, came as a surprise. Dawson didn't like surprises, especially the kind that made driving conditions hazardous.

On an oath, he returned to his bedroom, where he changed into more casual clothes than what he would have worn to the office. Then he headed back downstairs, brewed himself a second cup of coffee, and made his way to the study. As he always did on days when the weather was bad, he would work from home.

As a child, he'd loved the white stuff and not just because if enough of it fell, then he scored a day off from school. No, he'd loved playing in it, making forts out of it and packing it into balls for fights with his friends. As an adult he had not minded the snow, even when it created a headache during his commute to or from the office.

After the accident, however, he hated it and the ice it could conceal. The very sight of snow coating the roads caused his heart to race and his palms to sweat. His doctor told him that his physical symptoms were caused by anxiety. He'd even had a name for it: post-traumatic stress disorder. It didn't matter what label one attached to it. The result was the same. Dawson gave his driver the day off, secluded himself at home and worked remotely on days such as this.

Ingrid, his housekeeper, was more intrepid. Perhaps because she only lived a few miles away. She arrived this morning as he was finishing a Zoom meeting with Mrs. Stern, who also hadn't let the weather keep her from work. He instructed his assistant to field his calls and only forward those that were urgent. Everything else could wait until he returned to the office on Monday. As for Ingrid, other than inquiring if he would like more coffee, she left him alone. She'd been in his employ long enough to know his routine, even on rare days when he worked from home. She went about her business and left Dawson to his.

So, it came as a surprise when she tapped on his door late in the afternoon.

"Yes, Ingrid?" he asked when she poked her head around the door.

"I'm sorry to bother you, Mr. Burke," she apologized immediately. "But Eve Hawley is here to see you."

The leather chair creaked as he settled back in his seat. After what had happened—or rather what he *wanted* to happen—the other night, he shouldn't want to see Eve. And yet he did.

"Send her in, please."

Eve appeared in his doorway a moment later, smiling broadly and looking gorgeous enough to cause his breath to catch.

"Hey, Dawson. Sorry to bug you."

The woman had been a plague on his concentration the entire week, and yet seeing her in person—her face flushed from the cold, her hair ruffled by the wind—was exponentially more distracting.

Still, he managed to utter a casual, "That's all right." He rested his elbows on the desk blotter and steepled his fingers in front of him, summing up what he hoped was a bland expression even as his gaze continued to devour her. "Did we have an appointment?"

"No. Actually, I wasn't expecting to see you at all. I figured you would still be at your office."

Apparently, she had planned to avoid him just as he had avoided her all week. Once his ego absorbed that disappointment, he told her, "I decided to work from home today."

"So I see."

She came fully into the room then. Ingrid must have taken her coat. She wore an oversized cable-knit sweater and dark leggings that were tucked into a pair of high-heeled black leather boots that stopped just below the knee. Simple, casual. And incredibly appealing. As was that engaging smile of hers. His mouth went dry.

"What can I do for you, Eve?" he managed to ask, his tone curt.

He saw hurt flash in her dark eyes just before she blinked, and he hated himself for it. This wasn't her fault. What he was thinking, how he was feeling... none of this was her fault. At least not intentionally.

Her smile vanished, and the light went out of her eyes. When she spoke, her tone was all business.

"I have some gift ideas as well as some items I've already purchased for some of your family members. I was planning to leave them for you to look over, but when your housekeeper said you were here..." Her words trailed off and she shrugged.

Tell her you're sorry, his conscience commanded, but what came out of his mouth was, "Okay."

At his single, sparse word, she backed up a step, nodding as she went. None of the spunk she'd exhibited on her first visit to his home was evident when she said, "I'll leave everything with Ingrid and get out of your way. I can see you're busy. Sorry to have bothered you."

She turned and had gone before Dawson managed to hoist himself out of his chair. He caught up with her in the foyer just as she was pulling on her jacket.

"Eve, wait!"

She turned, a polite smile pulling up the corners of her mouth. "Yes?"

"Don't go. Please." He closed his eyes and shook his head. "Not like this."

"Like what?" She zipped up her jacket.

"Angry."

"I'm not angry, Dawson. Why in the world would I be angry?" she asked, punctuating her question by tossing the end of a scarf over one shoulder.

"Because I was being a jerk just now."

She stopped in the process of pulling on her gloves. "Yes," she agreed after a considering look. "You were. A rude jerk, to be precise."

Dawson's laughter was strained, even though she had broken the ice with her bluntness. He would rather she be angry with him than hurt. "You don't believe in cutting a guy any slack, do you?"

"To what purpose?"

He grimaced. Maybe angry wasn't so good after all. "Okay, how about this? Do you have any plans for dinner?"

"Tonight?" she inquired.

The woman was definitely playing hardball.

"Yes, tonight. I want to make up for the way I treated you just now. It's... it's been a bad day."

Her gaze softened, but then she tapped her lower

lip with the tip of her gloved index finger. "Hmm. Let me think. I don't have plans exactly, but I did take a chicken breast out of the freezer to thaw."

It was a bit of a blow to learn he could lose out to poultry. "Ingrid is making a pork roast."

"Ah, the other white meat," she said, jesting with an old industry slogan.

"Yes. She's a very good cook," he added in the hopes of aiding his cause.

Eve eyed him stoically for what felt like a lifetime before asking. "Do you *want* me to come to dinner, Dawson, or are you just feeling guilty?"

Of course she would cut right to the heart of the matter, he thought.

"I do and I am. Does that make a difference?"

"I guess one cancels out the other," she replied.

"Does that mean you accept my invitation?"

She tilted her head to one side. "It depends?"

"On what?"

"On what else is on the menu."

He cleared his throat. "I'm not sure. Probably some sort of rice or potato dish and a vegetable, I'd imagine. Ingrid is all about balanced meals," he said. And even though he knew he was babbling, he added, "She sometimes makes a side salad. Baby greens in this homemade vinaigrette. Do you have a preference? I can let Ingrid know and I'm sure she'll try to accommodate it."

"Actually, I meant in the way of conversation."

"Oh."

She folded her arms across her chest. "Are you going to talk to me?"

"Of course, I am," he replied, somewhat indignant, and pointed out the obvious. "I'm talking to you right now."

"I mean an actual conversation, Dawson. No chit-chat about the weather or diatribes on the economy. I can get that while watching the news as I eat my chicken."

He blew out a breath, wondering what had he just gotten himself into.

"You're a hard woman to please, Eve Hawley."

She unzipped the quilted down jacket she wore and laid it and the scarf over his arm. Her smile tripped up his pulse when she replied, "You don't know the half of it."

CHAPTER NINE

Since they had some time to kill before dinner was served, Dawson suggested they sit in the great room where a fire blazed cheerfully in the hearth. He helped Eve carry in the purchases she'd made. Given the volume, it was obvious she had been quite busy.

In the past, he had given Carole carte blanche to buy everything, including his family's gifts. Sometimes she would check in with him about a specific item. But mostly, Carole ran the show, which had been fine with him. Eve, of course, insisted on running everything past him.

"At the very least you should know what you bought so that when they thank you, you won't appear baffled."

Her logic made sense, but he replied, "I'm never baffled."

Her brows rose fractionally as if to say, "Right."

"Another one of your principles?" he asked.

"Exactly."

As they sat on the sofa and scoured through the items she had brought with her, Dawson was impressed. The woman certainly had a good eye. She had pegged his mother's taste perfectly with a specially designed amethyst ring that was surrounded by smaller stones. He didn't ask how she had managed to get it made so quickly. He figured the answer would come on his next credit card statement. But he didn't care about the cost. What mattered was that his mother was going to love it. He told Eve as much.

She smiled, looking pleased. "That was my thought, too. As for your dad..." She made a little humming noise. "He was difficult. I went out on a limb with this since it can't be returned, but since Clive seemed to be a real hockey fan, I thought he might appreciate it."

She pulled a red game jersey from the bag that was on her lap.

"That's Gordy Howe's number from his days with the Detroit Red Wings," Dawson said as he reached for it. "He was one of the all-time greats."

"It's a vintage National Hockey League sweater and it's signed. I know the Wings aren't your father's favorite team, but the Avalanche wasn't around back in the day." Her tone turned wry. "I only know this because I made a fool of myself in a store downtown that sells sports memorabilia."

Dawson laughed. "Dad's going to love it. He'll argue, of course, that Ted Lindsay was actually a better player than Howe, but he'll love it just the same. Thank you."

She rifled through another bag as he folded the jersey and set it aside.

"And here's the Misty Stark purse I mentioned getting for your sister. I went with something medium-sized from the designer's spring collection."

"Spring? As in *next* spring?"

"I know someone who knows someone who owes that someone a really big favor." She let out a sigh that was purely feminine. "Lisa's going to love it."

The handbag reminded Dawson of a pastel-colored sausage with handles. "I'll have to take your word for it," he said dryly.

"I'm still looking for something for your brother-in-law. Suggestions at this point would be appreciated. Christmas is less than two weeks away."

"I'll give it some thought," he replied.

"Maybe you could call your sister, pick her brain a little," she suggested. "Or you could go to Sunday dinner this weekend and talk to her there."

"I... I'll see what I can do."

"Okay. Thanks."

She showed him items she had purchased for Ingrid, Mrs. Stern, his driver, and some members of the senior management team at Burke Financial. After setting those aside, she leaned forward to pull a large and very heavy shopping bag across the Turkish rug. "And now for the *coup de grace*."

"What is it?"

"Take a peek."

Dawson felt a bit like a kid himself when he did. Inside was the gaming system Brian and Colton had been raving about the night of the ball.

"No way!" he said with a startled laugh. "I know you said you could get this for the boys, but... How on earth did you manage it?"

"Trade secret." She offered a cagey smile. "I can't give you specifics, but I can assure you that no laws were broken."

"The boys are going to love this." He grinned at her. "You're something else."

Eve focused her attention back on the bag. "I also picked up a few age-appropriate games to go with it that I think they will enjoy."

Of course she had. The woman was nothing if not thorough. "You think of everything."

"It's my job," she said lightly. "Besides, after the chemistry set fiasco, I felt you needed to really go all out to re-establish yourself as a 'cool' uncle."

He rubbed the back of his neck and offered a sheepish, "Thanks."

Although he'd known it all along, it hit him suddenly that he wouldn't be there to watch the boys open this gift. He wouldn't be there to see any of his family members open the thoughtful gifts Eve had picked out. Just as he hadn't been at his parents' house on Christmas Day last year or the year before.

As if she'd read his mind, Eve said, "It's a shame you won't be in town to see the boys tear into this. They're going to be so excited."

While his family gathered around a decorated real Douglas fir tree, joking, laughing, and exchanging presents, he would be alone in Cabo, as far away from snow and holiday merriment as he could possibly manage. Dawson pictured himself sitting poolside at the condo he'd rented, a tall glass of something chilled and fortified in one hand to help blot out the depressing memories.

Eve was watching him, apparently waiting for him to say something in response. He gave a negligent shrug. "I'll catch up with them after the holidays."

He always did. After the new year he would clear a day on his calendar to hang out with just the boys, spoiling them rotten. And he would schedule an evening out with his sister and brother-in-law, picking up the tab at some swanky restaurant and paying for their sitter. And, finally, he would make plans with his parents, usually a weekend evening at his home, where he would pay Ingrid double her usual wage to prepare a sizable feast and clean up afterward.

All of this because of the guilt he felt for skipping Christmas. And yet none of it doing a blessed thing to move the needle on his conscience.

"Okay. Terrific." She nodded. He didn't trust her easy agreement and for good reason. "You can see them at a Sunday dinner after the holidays at your parents' house."

"Eve—"

She cut him off by slapping her knee in an exaggerated fashion. "Oh, wait, I forgot. You don't go to Sunday dinners at your parents' house any longer."

"Are you trying to make me feel bad?" he asked tightly. "I can assure you, there's no need. I already do."

Instead of apologizing, Eve said, "Good, then you understand exactly how your loved ones feel when you shut them out and stand them up not just on the holidays but on a regular basis throughout the year."

On an oath, he launched to his feet. Irritation and guilt blended together, proving to be a volatile mix. "Didn't your mother ever tell you that it's not polite to poke around in people's private affairs?" he snapped.

"No. She didn't." Eve stood as well. "My mother died of a drug overdose when I was eight."

He blanched. "Eve, I... I didn't know. I'm sorry."

"No." She kneaded her forehead. "I'm sorry. I played that like a damned trump card, and it was a lousy thing to do. But I'm not sorry for poking around in your private affairs, as you put it."

"Why does this matter to you?" he demanded.

"Because... because it..." Her next words nipped his anger in the bud. "Because *you* matter to me, Dawson. Okay? You matter."

"Eve." He closed his eyes and shook his head, unable or unwilling to process the emotions her words evoked. Or maybe he was just too afraid. After all, it was hard to cling tightly to the past when a part of him wanted to reach for the future.

"I probably shouldn't tell you that," she said quietly. He opened his eyes in time to watch her swallow and cross her arms over her chest. The move struck him as defensive rather than defiant, especially when she added, "Unfortunately, I have a very bad habit of leading with my heart where men are concerned. Just don't let it go to your head."

"I don't know what to say," he replied, although the truth was that Eve mattered to him, too. In a very short amount of time, she had managed to thoroughly shake up the status quo of Dawson's otherwise rigidly ordered life. He still wasn't sure he liked it. It left him feeling so unsettled.

"Don't say anything. I prefer to do all the talking anyway." She pushed the hair back from her face and expelled a deep breath. "As my bombshell of a moment ago should make perfectly clear to you, I don't come from the kind of family you do. After my mother died, my father took off and I was shuttled around from one relative to another, all of whom made it perfectly clear that they disapproved of my dad, had been disappointed in my mother, and didn't have very high hopes that I'd amount to much."

"Aw, Eve."

"Don't feel sorry for me. That's not the purpose behind my words. You're lucky, Dawson. *Very* lucky to have people who care about you and who want to remain close to you."

"I know I'm lucky. I do. But I am sorry about what happened to you."

"Don't be. I've accepted my family for what it is and my father for what he isn't. He's let grief and regret rule and ruin his life. I don't want to see you make the same mistake." She blinked a couple of times in rapid succession, her eyes bright with unshed tears. But then she managed a smile and said brightly, "Okay, that's all I'm going to say on either subject."

Dawson didn't quite believe her. But before he could think of an appropriate response to everything she had just shared, Ingrid cleared her throat from the doorway.

"Dinner is ready, Mr. Burke."

. . .

Dawson's formal dining room sported vaulted ceilings, a crystal chandelier and an oval cherry table that could comfortably accommodate a dozen guests. Another gas fireplace and a centerpiece of fresh flowers and glowing candles made the large room cozy. But it was the framed family portrait hanging over the mantle that made it personal.

Eve had never seen photographs of Dawson's late wife and daughter, but even if he hadn't been included in the shot, she would have known who the other two people were. In an odd way, she recognized them, even if she did not recognize the happy, relaxed man who was seated with them.

As Ingrid set out serving dishes heaped with steaming food, Eve discreetly studied the photograph. Sheila was blond-haired and blue-eyed with the delicate beauty of a porcelain doll. Isabelle was lovely, too. Eve glimpsed mischief in the little girl's light eyes and a hint of her father's stubbornness in her small jaw. She'd expected them to be beautiful and they were. But what truly surprised Eve was the odd connection she felt to Dawson's loved ones and the disappointment that they would never meet.

The dinner conversation started out stilted and strained thanks to the emotionally charged discussion that had preceded it. She blamed herself for that. What had she been thinking, provoking the man and then essentially baring her soul to him? She didn't want his pity any more than he wanted hers.

No matter. The deed was done and it was pointless to waste her time or energy regretting it now. Besides, she had spoken the truth. Dawson *did* matter to her. Eve hadn't even realized how much until the words tumbled out of her mouth.

Oh, well. She was who she was, although it seemed she never learned. She picked up stakes and started over, but she never learned.

Eve was fussing with her napkin when Dawson asked, "Would you like some wine?"

They were seated opposite one another at the far end of the table. She pushed her glass closer to him. "Yes, but just half a glass, please."

Once he'd poured the chilled pinot grigio, dinner became a far more relaxed affair. It had nothing to do with the loosening effects of alcohol, but rather the fact that Dawson spilled his wine down the front of his shirt when he went to take a sip.

It was unintentional, of that Eve was sure. He wasn't the sort of man given to slapstick comedy, although he had relaxed considerably since their first meeting. Had that been mere weeks ago? But the mishap added some much-needed levity.

"I can't believe I just did that," he muttered as he dabbed the front of his shirt with his napkin. "Good thing it's white wine."

"It's my fault," Eve said.

He stopped blotting and glanced over at her. "How do you figure that?"

Straight-faced, she replied, "It's the effect I have on men. They become blundering fools in my presence."

Dawson snorted. And even though he was smiling, he sounded somewhat serious when he replied, "You certainly do have an effect on me, Eve."

Half an hour later, Eve pushed back from the table with a contented sigh. "I probably should have passed on that second helping of tenderloin, but it was too good."

"Irresistible," he agreed as he watched Eve dab her mouth with a linen napkin.

Heat curled inside her at the remark, which was only suggestive because of his expression. Just over his right shoulder, Sheila and Isabelle smiled down at Eve from the portrait, dousing any flames before they could start. Just as well, she decided.

During the meal, while they'd talked companionably, steering clear of weighty or emotionally charged topics, it had grown dark outside and the candles in the centerpiece had burned low. Even though Eve planned to leave as soon as good manners would allow once they'd finished eating, she glanced out the window and re-evaluated.

"How about we go outside for a walk, work off some of these calories," she suggested. She had limited herself to that single half-glass of wine, but she figured the fresh air would be good for her head as well.

"A walk? It's snowing," he said.

"Yes, Captain Obvious, I hear it does that a lot in Denver. No need to worry. I won't melt." Her eyebrows arched. "Or are you afraid that you will?"

"It's getting dark, Eve."

Dawson's house was surrounded by a private, almost park-like setting with mature trees and meandering paths. She had admired it since her first visit to his home. "Your landscape lighting looks adequate enough for a leisurely stroll."

But he wasn't done arguing. "The paths haven't been shoveled recently. A good three inches have fallen since the grounds crew went through last."

She batted that excuse aside, too.

"That's all right. I'm wearing boots." Of course, the boots in question were unlined and made of supple Italian leather with three-inch heels that hardly made them suitable for a hike—or even a stroll—in inclement weather, but she was willing to take her chances. "You do own a pair, right?"

"I don't know."

"You don't know if you have boots?"

"I don't know about going outside."

Like a veteran poker player, Eve upped the ante. "I promise to protect you."

But it was Dawson who called. "Maybe I'm not the one who needs protecting."

"Is that a threat?" she inquired.

He set aside his napkin and pushed back from the table. Gaze direct and challenging, he said, "That snow is perfect for packing."

She liked this playful side of Dawson. "Are you suggesting a snowball fight?"

"There's only one way to find out. Are you still game for that walk?"

"Please." She snorted. "Your question is insulting. I've never backed down from a challenge."

"I didn't think you had." One side of his mouth lifted, tugging her pulse rate right along with it. "I'll get our coats."

Outside, the air was crisp. It stole Eve's breath, making her glad for the scarf that she'd wound around her neck. She tucked her chin into it now.

"It's really beautiful out here," she commented. And it was. Winter had wrought its magic, covering everything in a pristine layer of white that sparkled like diamonds in the landscaping lights.

"The grounds were what attracted me to this property in the first place," Dawson admitted.

"I can see why."

"If you think it's beautiful now, you should see it in the spring and summer. The flowerbeds are incredible, and there's a koi pond that has lily pads."

"I wouldn't have taken you for a green thumb."

"Oh, it's black, believe me. I know my limits, which is why I hired the services of a professional."

She grinned. "The economy loves people who know their limits, since it helps create all sorts of job opportunities."

"Like professional shoppers?"

"Exactly."

"Well, I'm glad to do my part for my country." His voice grew soft, almost reverent, when he said, "You know, I haven't walked out here in the winter in... a long time."

Eve figured she knew exactly how long, so she remained silent.

After a moment, he added, "I used to love winter. I looked forward to the first snowfall."

"Me, too." She scuffed the toe of her boot along the walkway, ruffling the blanket of white, before bending down to scoop up a handful. "Snow makes everything seem so clean, so perfect," she told him as she compacted the snow into a ball.

"And your life wasn't perfect."

"Nope. But whose is?" She shrugged off the melancholy of childhood memories and changed the subject. "You know, you were right about this being good packing snow."

"So I see. Are you thinking of making a snowman or something?"

"Or something." When she smiled, his eyes narrowed.

"You know, I've changed my mind. I don't think a snowball fight would be such a good idea."

"Afraid you'll lose?" she asked in challenge.

"No." He smiled now. "But you're a guest and I'd hate to show you up."

"Please," she scoffed and levered back her arm.

He backed up a couple of steps "Eve, I mean it. You don't want to do that."

But he was still smiling. And he looked younger and all the more handsome for it.

"And if I do?"

"You do and you'll be asking for trouble."

"Dawson, Dawson," Eve chided, shaking her head. "What did I tell you about me and challenges?"

"That you never back—" The snowball hit him in the chest before he could finish. He gaped at her. "I can't believe you just did that."

Eve bent down and scooped up a second handful. "Then this is going to come as a complete shock," she replied, tossing the loosely packed snow right into his face.

Her laughter followed the ball's flight path, but her mirth was short lived. Dawson didn't even pause to wipe the snow off before he launched himself in her direction. She feinted right and then went left to avoid him, laughing like crazy, and managed to get a full ten feet up the path before he caught up with her and grabbed her around her waist.

"You're in for it—"

His words were choked off when Eve began to fall, betrayed by her impractical boots. Both she and

Dawson went down hard, but the snow helped cushion her fall. The snow and the man. Somehow, he had managed to turn his body at the last moment so that she wound up partially on top of him.

"Are you okay?" he asked, sounding as winded as she felt.

"I think I broke my heel," she managed to wheeze out.

He swore softly. "Are you in pain?"

Eve laughed as she clarified, "The heel of my boot. I think it got caught in between the pavers. What were you doing, anyway, grabbing me from behind? We were supposed to be having a snowball fight."

"We still are."

With that he brought up his snow-filled hand and rubbed it over her cheek. It wasn't only the cold that had her shivering. Dawson had shifted their positions so that now he was on top of her.

"You know, when I was a kid, I didn't believe in taking any prisoners. But I've decided to make an exception in your case. You're too pretty to annihilate."

"So, I'm your prisoner."

"Yes."

"Hmm." She made a considering face. "I guess this isn't so bad."

"That's because the torture hasn't begun yet." His gaze was on her lips.

"Torture?" she repeated in a husky voice she barely recognized as her own. "What kind of torture?"

"This," he whispered, just before his mouth met hers.

CHAPTER TEN

Dawson could think of a million reasons why he should stop the kiss before it progressed any further. First among them was the fact that he and Eve were outside lying on the snow-covered ground. Apparently, she didn't mind. Even though she was shivering, when he started to pull away, she wrapped her arms around his neck and held him in place, taking from him where a moment ago she had been the one giving.

Her arms weren't the only things wrapped around him. Her legs were, too. One was hooked over his calf, the other angled up over his thigh, anchoring him in place. Their bodies fit together perfectly. He could tell that despite the layers of their clothes, and it fueled both his imagination and his desire.

It had been a long time–a very long time—since he'd laid atop a woman. His body had no trouble remembering the pleasure. No trouble at all. Need surged through him with tsunami force, shredding his control until it hung by a thread. Although Dawson knew he was playing with fire, he rocked forward slightly anyway.

Eve moaned.

He did it again.

This time they both moaned, and that last frayed thread of his control snapped. It was only when the cold leather of Eve's gloved hands moved beneath his jacket and sweater and came into contact with the bare skin just above the waistband of his jeans that reality came slamming back.

"This is insane," he managed as he came up for air.

There didn't seem to be enough of it, especially when he glanced down at Eve. She looked like something out of a fantasy, lying in the snow with her dark hair splayed out around her head. Despite the low light, her eyes glowed with an intoxicating mix of awareness and humor.

"Absolutely insane," she agreed with a laugh. "My butt is numb."

Parts of Dawson had lost all feeling, too. Unfortunately, his back wasn't one of them. He discovered this when he levered away from Eve and rolled to one side. Long into the night, and in more ways than one, he would be paying for this spontaneous and very sensual tussle.

Grimacing as he rose, he reached down to help Eve to her feet.

"Are you okay?" she asked.

"I will be." After a couple or four painkillers. He'd also be calling Wanda for a therapeutic massage first thing in the morning.

They entered the house through the French doors that led from the patio directly into the kitchen. Eve had limped, thanks to her broken boot heel. Dawson always hated entering the house in the evening after Ingrid had gone home. Even though he liked his privacy, the place was so quiet and seemed so... lifeless. Eve chased away the gloom when she stamped her feet—albeit awkwardly—and gave her damp hair a toss.

"Ingrid's no longer here, but I can make some coffee or a cup of tea, if you'd like," he offered.

"Oh, your housekeeper doesn't live here?"

"No."

"What about your driver?" she asked.

"Since I need him to be on call, his rooms are over the garage."

"Ah, and that masseuse I saw the first day we met?" she asked as she removed her scarf and unzipped her jacket.

He chuckled ruefully. "At the moment, I wish Wanda lived here, but no. I like my privacy."

"Nothing wrong with privacy," she murmured in agreement. After tucking her scarf into the sleeve of her jacket, she draped it around the back of one chair, which she then pulled out from the table and sank down on with a heavy sigh. "Do you have any hot chocolate?"

"I... honestly don't know. Possibly."

"I'd prefer that to tea or coffee, if you have it. Chocolate in any form beats all else," she informed him.

"I believe my sister has made that very claim."

"I knew I liked her." Then, "Ooh, and hot chocolate needs to have little marshmallows. I love those little marshmallows."

"Are you talking about those miniscule dehydrated ones that taste like cardboard?"

"Sure. They're an integral part of the experience. And they don't taste like cardboard once they start to melt into the hot chocolate." She grinned.

Her childlike enthusiasm when it came to life's simple pleasures was addictive. Dawson realized he was grinning, too.

"I can't make any promises, but I'll do my best to accommodate your request. In the meantime, we probably should get out of our wet clothes."

"Hmm." She tapped her bowed lips with an index finger.

"What?" he asked as he draped his coat over the back of another chair.

"I'm trying to decide if you're being chivalrous with that suggestion or merely clever," Eve said.

He smiled, enjoying their banter. "A man can be both."

"Okay, you can prove that by helping me out of these boots. The leather is wet and they feel like they've become a second skin." She smiled up at him, managing to look both prim and provocative.

He knelt because it was warranted and reached for the zipper on the side of the boot. The leather was high quality and soaked to the ankle. He had a bad feeling her boots were ruined, and not just because of the broken heel.

"These aren't exactly practical footwear for Denver winters," he said.

"No, but they sure are sexy."

She had a point. It took a little effort, but Dawson managed to free the boot from her foot. Though she hadn't asked him to, he peeled off the damp stocking beneath it, revealing a set of chilly pink toes whose nails were painted fire engine red. He rubbed the foot between his hands, chafing some warmth into it and hoping to cool down his libido in the process. Since his first days of dating, he'd had a thing for red toenails on women. He wasn't sure why. Something about it was so provocative. That was especially true in the winter when no one else was likely to see them. It made this glimpse more intimate, almost like a secret.

He groaned.

"Is your back giving you trouble?" Eve asked,

sounding concerned. "I wasn't thinking when I asked you to help me. I can probably do this myself."

He pushed her hands away.

"Oh, no." He moved on to the other foot. "I'm fine."

Dawson was one-hundred and eighty degrees from fine, but he didn't want to deny himself a single second of this sweet torture. So he performed the same ministrations on the second foot as he had on the first. And, even though he knew the nails on its toes would also be painted red, he felt a potent kick of lust when he slipped off her stocking and saw them.

Afterward, he put her boots on the mat where he'd left his own soggy loafers.

"I have a robe you can put on while your clothes are in the dryer."

"What? You're not offering to help me off with those, too?" she tempted, arching one eyebrow.

There were a few ways Dawson could answer her question. What he chose was, "If I do, will you return the favor?"

She gave him a knowing look, but said nothing.

Sweeping his arm, he said, "Right this way."

Eve followed him down the hall, past the formal dining room that Ingrid had put to rights during their time outside. Then past the tidy great room and

Dawson's well-ordered study. She'd seen some of the rooms earlier today and on a previous visit, but she was curious about the rest of the house. People's homes said a lot about them. Dawson's told of a fondness for fine things. All of the rooms were large and lushly appointed. She wouldn't call the furnishings fussy or ornate, but they were definitely high quality. And everything was immaculate.

The bedrooms were located on the second floor, up a staircase that curved dramatically around the two-story foyer. Her nerves were humming along on high by the time they reached the master suite.

To one side of the room was a fireplace with its own cozy sitting area. She chose to concentrate on it rather than the king-sized bed. With the touch of a few buttons, flames shot to life and soft lighting illuminated the room's periphery.

"I think your bedroom is bigger than my entire apartment," Eve remarked as Dawson disappeared into the walk-in closet. He emerged a moment later with a sumptuous terrycloth robe in one hand and a fresh change of clothes for himself in the other.

"Here you go," he said, handing her the robe. "You can change in there. The bathroom is right through that door." He backed up a step, looking endearingly flustered when he added, "I'll just... um... use one of the rooms down the hall."

"Should I meet you downstairs afterward?"

"Sure. I'll start the cocoa."

"Don't forget the marshmallows," she called just before he closed the door.

Once alone, Eve made fast work of changing her clothes. She was full-out shivering now, gooseflesh puckering her skin. Cold was the culprit rather than all those desperate feelings Dawson inspired. Still, she wanted to blush when she recalled the crazy way she had clung to him out in the snow. She hadn't wanted to let go, because she knew once she did, he would retreat again to that isolated prison he'd constructed for himself out of guilt and grief. To her surprise, however, he hadn't withdrawn completely, even if his emotions were once again under control.

It was a pity, she thought. She had enjoyed those brief glimpses of the man he most likely had been before the accident. Happy, funny… fun.

Could he be that man again? Did he want to be?

The robe was too big. No surprise there, but the fact that it smelled like him had her insides coiling into knots. Eve turned up the sleeves and cinched the belt as tightly as she could, knotting it just to be on the safe side before gathering up her damp garments and returning downstairs. She found Dawson in the kitchen, standing in front of the six-burner gas stove. He was stirring a pan of milk. He glanced up at her arrival.

She suddenly felt shy. "Hi."

He was dressed in jeans and a chambray shirt, which he'd left untucked. It was the most casual she'd ever seen him, and by far the most domestic. The wealthy and resourceful Dawson Burke was heating milk to make hot cocoa.

"Hi." His gaze connected with hers before meandering down to her bare feet, and she saw him swallow before he looked away. "I should have thought to give you a pair of socks."

"Nah. I'll be fine, especially if I can prop my feet up in front of a fireplace. There doesn't seem to be any shortage of those in your house."

"No. This place has four. All of them are gas."

She motioned to the burner. "You might want to lower the heat or you'll scald the milk."

He did as she suggested and then motioned for her to come closer. "Why don't you take over stirring while I throw your things in the dryer?"

"Are you sure you know how to operate one of those?" she asked wryly.

"I think I can figure it out." Tongue in cheek, he added, "Of course, that's assuming I can remember where the laundry room is."

She laughed and handed over her leggings and socks. "Only the back hem of my sweater was damp and, since it's wool, I left it to dry in front of the fireplace in your room along with some of the, um, more delicate items."

His Adam's apple bobbed a second time. "Okay."

When he continued to stand rooted in place

staring at her, Eve added, "The regular setting on the dryer is fine for those."

Dawson cleared his throat. "Regular setting. Got it."

Dawson took his time in the laundry room, collecting his thoughts and trying to reel in his desire. The woman in his kitchen was wearing his bathrobe—and not much else. His mind kept returning to that inconvenient fact.

Where was this heading? Where did he *want* it to head? The questions tumbled in his head as Eve's clothes began to tumble in the dryer. He was no closer to an answer when he returned to the kitchen a few minutes later.

"Cocoa's ready," she informed him. "I mixed in the chocolate syrup while you were gone. No marshmallows, I see."

"No. Sorry."

She shrugged. "I'm just impressed you had a bottle of Hershey's in your fridge."

"I think it's from the last time my nephews came over. My sister brought all the makings for ice cream sundaes."

"When was that?"

He frowned, thinking back. "The summer before last."

"Well, I guess it's a good thing that stuff has a long shelf life."

They took their mugs to the sitting room where Eve had sipped a cup of tea during her first visit to Dawson's home. He started the fire with a push of a button as she lowered herself to the rug just in front of the hearth and put her feet as close to the flames as possible.

"Mmm," she murmured with a sigh. "This feels wonderful." Dawson was still standing, mug in hand. Eve glanced up at him. "Aren't you going to sit down?"

"Yes, but I was planning to use a chair."

"Why would you do that when there's a perfectly good patch of floor right here?"

She patted said patch. But her smile turned the benign gesture into a dare. Dawson grabbed a couple of throw pillows off the sofa and tossed them in her direction. Then he joined her, proving to them both that Eve wasn't the only one who refused to back down from a challenge.

"So, how's the cocoa?" he asked.

She took a sip, leaving a fine layer of froth on her upper lip, which she promptly licked off. "I've had better."

He resisted the urge to groan, but not the urge to touch her. "You've still got a little…" He traced her top lip with the tip of his index finger, pretending to brush away a nonexistent smudge.

"All gone?" she asked.

"I think so." Still staring at her mouth, he said, "Sorry that I couldn't find any marshmallows to go in it."

"That's all right." Her lips curved. "It was a tall order. You don't strike me as the sort of man who drinks hot chocolate with little marshmallows."

He shook his head. "Not often, no."

"Of course, you didn't strike me as the sort who would tackle me in the snow, either."

"I didn't tackle you. I tried to break your fall," he said.

"Yes, but I only fell because you chased me."

"I only chased you because you threw a snowball at me. Two, in fact," he reminded her. "And I did give you fair warning before you fired the second one."

She took another sip of the cocoa and gave him a curious glance. "Okay. I'll give you that. Of course, I'm going to want a rematch. And the next time I can promise you I won't be wearing a pair of high-heeled boots that are far more suited to fashion than they are to function."

"Too bad. I really like those boots." He tortured himself with a glance at her bare feet.

"I loved them." Her lips pursed. "They are... were my favorite. They're probably ruined now, especially since I busted the heel."

"I'll buy you another pair," he offered magnanimously.

"That's very nice of you, but there's no need. It was my own fault."

"Agreed," Dawson said and enjoyed watching her scowl at him. "So, what will you wear for our rematch?"

"A pair of waterproof hikers, my ski bibs, and a down parka."

"You ski?" he asked, marginally surprised.

"Not really, but I look absolutely amazing in the outfit. Like something out of a magazine." She winked.

Dawson didn't laugh, even though she had obviously intended the description as a joke. Rather, he replied solemnly, "I don't doubt it. I'm beginning to think you would look amazing in just about anything."

He allowed his gaze to skim over the curves that were mostly obscured by thick folds of his terrycloth robe. Amazing.

"I... I... Hmm," was all she managed to say in response.

Dawson rather liked knowing that he had made Eve tongue-tied, since the woman had had that effect on him more than once during the past couple of weeks. And then, even though he knew he was playing with fire, he told her, "I really like what you have on at the moment."

She coughed and recovered enough to joke, "What? This old thing?"

"You know, I never really cared for that robe... until now."

For that matter, he knew he'd never put it on again without thinking about Eve and remembering just how provocative she looked with firelight and curiosity dancing in her eyes.

"I'll take that as a compliment."

He set aside his mug. She followed suit.

"You should," he said.

The space between them diminished fractionally with each breath they took until their faces were nearly touching. She smelled like chocolate, and he was eager to taste it, but he knew that wasn't the reason he suddenly felt so starved.

He ran his fingers through the loose tumble of her curls. "Your hair is still damp," he murmured.

"Dawson." Eve sighed his name, closed her eyes, and just that fast he knew he was doomed. But as he followed her down onto the fire-warmed rug, it felt far more like a resurrection than it did an execution.

He started at her neck, nibbling the spot just below her jaw where he could feel her pulse beating.

Life. It was right there under his lips, inviting him, enticing him to return to the land of the living. And so he moved lower, alternately kissing and nipping his way to her collar bone. Her skin was soft and as smooth as satin. When he pushed the robe off her shoulder, her skin all but glowed in the firelight.

He glanced up to find Eve watching him. Her expression was more serious than he had ever seen her. Those beautiful dark eyes were wide and still filled with questions. Dawson wasn't sure he could give her any of the answers she sought. Come right down to it, he had plenty of questions himself.

He started with the most pressing.

"Are you sure?" he whispered.

She hesitated only a moment, but it seemed an eternity. When she finally nodded, he stood and helped her to her feet. They didn't speak a word as, hands clasped, he led her through the quiet house back upstairs to his bedroom.

CHAPTER ELEVEN

Eve awoke to blaring classic rock and a man's heavy arm draped possessively over her waist.

She smiled at the ceiling in Dawson's bedroom as waves of contentment rushed over her. Life was good.

The electric guitar was gearing up for its solo before Dawson finally stirred. He reached out a hand to swat off the alarm clock that was on the bedside table. The only problem was that Eve was in the way. His eyes opened as he realized this. His gaze was bleary at first and then clouded with what she recognized as desire.

Oh, yeah. Life was good.

She stroked his cheek, made scratchy from a night's growth of beard, and reveled in the distinctively masculine feel. "Good morning."

"That remains to be seen."

"Oh?"

He rolled on top of her and murmured something into her hair that she couldn't quite decipher. Not that it really mattered. Words weren't necessary at that moment. Eve understood Dawson's meaning perfectly.

An hour later, they were both out of bed and she had showered and was dressed. Thankfully, Dawson had found a new toothbrush for her in his linen closet, and Eve kept some makeup essentials in her purse. Without the taming effect of a flat iron, however, her hair had gone from pleasantly wavy to a riot of tangled curls, but there was no help for that. She brushed it back as best she could and tucked it behind her ears.

Her clothes had dried and were waiting for her on the chair in the bedroom when came out of the bathroom. Dawson had even brought her boots up from downstairs. The leather was no longer wet but it was definitely trashed. Still, she laughed when she realized that he had made them wearable by breaking off the other heel. At least she wouldn't be limping when she did the walk of shame to her Tahoe. Of course, it was Saturday, which meant Dawson's housekeeper had the day off, so there was no one here to see said walk and, besides, shame wasn't what Eve was feeling. Only happiness. Pure, unfiltered, undiluted happiness.

She dressed and, satisfied that she looked

presentable, ambled downstairs. She planned to just grab a cup of coffee and be on her way. It might be the weekend, but she had a busy day of shopping ahead of her. Some very good sales were going on, and even though she did a lot of her purchasing online these days, there was something exhilarating about pressing through throngs of shoppers to score a good deal as Christmas music blared over the loudspeakers. But her plans changed when she found Dawson in the kitchen.

He looked every bit as sexy as he had when he'd smiled at her first thing that morning and initiated another round of love-making. With minimal effort and very few words, he now talked her into staying for breakfast. He stood in front of the six-burner gas cook top like a captain standing at the helm of a ship.

Eve took in the array of ingredients and utensils spread out on the counter around him. Her tone was dubious when she asked, "Can you actually cook or is all this just for show?"

He looked mildly insulted. "I went away to college. I lived in a fraternity house with nine guys."

"So, we're having pizza and beer for breakfast?" she asked dryly.

"I can manage an omelet."

"Sorry. I don't know what I was thinking, questioning your culinary abilities. I mean, you did whip up that hot cocoa last night. Oh, wait, that's right. You just heated the milk and left the rest to me."

"Smart ass." He motioned toward one of the stools on the opposite side of the marble-topped island. "Go sit down before I rescind the invitation."

She sent him a two-fingered salute and did as he asked.

She had to admit, Dawson was reasonably proficient in the kitchen for a man who was used to having others do the cooking for him. He mastered the eggs—scrambled, although they had started out over easy—and the toast was salvageable once Eve scraped the worst of the burned edges off with a knife before buttering it. The coffee was more than good, excellent in fact. But she suspected that out of all the high-end appliances in Dawson's state-of-the-art kitchen, that one was probably the one he operated most frequently.

She ate the eggs, nibbled on half a piece of the burned toast, and helped herself to a second cup of the freshly ground dark roast.

Sunshine streamed in through the French doors and from the large window over the sink, making the room bright and inviting. She studied her surroundings, taking in the gleaming, professional-grade appliances, white cabinetry, and marble countertops. "I've got to tell you. This is a wonderful kitchen, a chef's dream," she told him. "I think you have more shelf space in your sub-zero refrigerator than I have in my entire kitchen."

"Thank you. Sheila—" He stopped himself.

"I bet she was a good cook," Eve said.

"Yes." He took a sip of his coffee. "How about you? Can you cook?"

"Yes. I went away to college, too," she teased. Between student loans and scholarships, Eve had managed four years at a state university. "I wanted to major in fashion design, but the school didn't offer that degree program. It was just as well. I figured out pretty quickly that I preferred shopping for clothes to making them."

"I think you made a smart career choice."

"I did," she agreed and took another sip of her coffee. "Anyway, I lived in an apartment just off campus with three other girls. We were all pretty decent cooks. We just couldn't afford much in the way of ingredients."

"Boxed mac and cheese?" he asked, forking up the last of his eggs.

"And canned soup."

"What about ramen noodles?"

She grinned. "Those too. They're a college staple. But these days I get to practice my culinary skills on a regular basis."

"You cook for yourself every night?" He looked impressed.

"Not every night," she admitted. "I have a pretty close relationship with a Chinese restaurant that's up the block from my apartment. It's the only phone number I know off the top of my head."

"I think I'm insulted."

"Don't be. It goes without saying that after last night I'll memorize yours now, too," she assured him, leaning over to kiss his cheek.

Dawson stiffened and cleared his throat. In the blink of an eye, his expression shuttered and Eve's heart sank. She knew what he was about to say even before he began speaking. Her sudden clairvoyance, however, did little to soften the impact.

"About last night, Eve. I hope you're not... I mean, I hope you understand that I'm not... Well, I'm not looking for something serious right now," he finally managed to say. "And the thing is, I may never be."

"Define serious."

"You know what I mean."

"Apparently I don't." She pushed her plate aside and folded her arms over her chest. Beneath them, she swore her heart felt bruised. "Why don't you enlighten me?"

"Eve, I like you. I like you *a lot*. That should be obvious. But I can't..." He shoved a hand through his hair and expelled a frustrated breath. "I just... can't."

"Actually, you can and you did. Very well, I might add," she told him, being intentionally obtuse. "Twice last night and then again this morning."

She wanted to rewind time, but since that was impossible, she would settle for seeing him smile. She wanted the funny, relaxed Dawson back. But he was dead serious when he replied, "I'm not talking about physically."

No. Of course he wasn't. "Which leaves emotionally," she said.

He nodded and she felt her heart go from bruised to fractured. For the first time since he had led her upstairs, Eve wondered if she had made a huge mistake. To think that just an hour ago she had greeted the morning with a smile and thought her life was grand.

Because far more than her pride was stinging at the moment, she told him, "I don't believe I mentioned expecting to march down a church aisle wearing white anytime soon."

"No. But I need to be sure that you understand where I'm coming from."

She swallowed, raised her chin. "I believe I do. You're saying that our relationship is temporary."

"Temporary is not the word I would have chosen," he said quietly.

"Semantics aside, it's what you mean. What's going on between us, well, ultimately, it's not going anywhere."

Dawson looked miserable. He looked remorseful. But he didn't contradict her.

You're just not good enough.

The words echoed in her head, taunting her. It seemed to be the motto for her life, the tagline that summed it up. She hadn't been good enough for her ex-boyfriend's well-to-do family. And now she wasn't good enough to compete with Dawson's memories of his late wife and the previous life he had enjoyed as a husband and father.

"I'm sorry, Eve."

Far from being appreciated, his apology only made her feel worse. Around the lump in her throat she said, "I want to be sure that you understand something. I'm not the sort of woman who just hops into bed with a guy on a whim."

"I know that—"

"No." She slashed a hand through the air to silence him. "This obviously needs to be said after what happened last night. When I'm with a man, I'm not just marking time until something or someone better comes along."

"I'm not marking time, Eve. I promise you that."

No. She knew that. How could he when he was stuck in the past? But she needed to be clear.

"Also, when I'm in a relationship I'm exclusive and I expect the same in return. Nothing about me is casual, Dawson, if you follow my meaning."

"I do."

"Good. I stayed here with you last night because being with you *meant* something to me." Her eyes filled with tears, and she hated herself for the weakness they represented, especially given their futility. But she blinked them away and pressed on. She would have her say now. A good cry could wait until later. "I stayed here because *you* mean something to me."

He stroked her cheek with his fingertips. "Eve, I know that. I would know that even without you saying it."

"We slept together, and it was amazing," she admitted. "But I'm not expecting a marriage proposal. I learned to manage my expectations after Drew. Truthfully, I don't know what I'm expecting anymore, except for the other person—you in this case—to be honest with me and monogamous for as long as, well, for as long as whatever this is lasts."

Her anger and indignation were spent. She wanted them back, because insecurity had begun filling the void.

"You have both," he promised. Then, "And for the record, I'm not the casual sort either."

She nodded and pushed back her stool so she could stand. Gathering up what remained of her pride, she forced a smile to her lips. "Well. Thank you for breakfast this morning and dinner last night."

"Wait. You're leaving right now?" He frowned.

"Yeah. I need to be going." *Before I make a bigger fool of myself.*

"Eve." Dawson put a hand on her arm to stop her as she started to turn away. There really was no need, as his next words rooted her in place. "I want you to know that since my wife died, you're the first woman

I've been with. You're the first woman I've even *wanted* to be with."

She closed her eyes and tried to steel her heart, but how could she not tumble a little further into love with this man after he made such a soul-baring admission?

"Oh, Dawson." She turned to fully face him, framed his face in her hands, and kissed him tenderly. "Thank you for telling me that."

"You're special to me," he whispered. "Please don't doubt that."

"Okay." But inside her head, a small voice kept asking: *Am I special enough to make you let go of the past and start thinking about the future?* She ignored it, stepped back and tugged at the hem of her sweater. "I really do need to be going."

"You're not working today, are you? It's Saturday."

"I know. But that's when the sales start. And there's a great one today at Macy's that has already been going on for an hour." She worked up a smile. "I love spending your money, Dawson, but I do try to save my clients a little whenever I can."

He smiled back. "Then I suppose I should thank you for staying with me as long as you have."

He helped her into her jacket and pulled on his coat so he could walk her out to the Tahoe. Then he insisted on brushing the snow from her windows while she sat in the driver's seat and let the vents blast her with cold air. When he finished, he stopped at her window and waited for her to roll it down so he could hand her the scraper.

"Thanks."

His brows were drawn together in worry when he said, "The roads might still be bad."

"I'll be careful."

He leaned in and awkwardly kissed her through the window. Afterward, he stuffed his hands in his pockets. He exhaled and the chilly air wreathed in white around his face.

"You're going to be okay, Dawson," she said and rolled up the window.

As she idled the Tahoe down the drive, Eve wondered if she would be.

―――

The house seemed especially quiet after Eve left and empty in a way it hadn't been while she had been in it. Dawson felt empty, too. This emptiness was different than how he'd felt for the past three years and, oddly, less easy to accept. Perhaps because he didn't have to. He had a choice. But he wasn't sure he wanted to have a choice. He wasn't sure he warranted one.

Restless, he spent the next few hours wandering from room to room. Reminders of Sheila and Isabelle were everywhere in the house. His daughter had taken her first steps in the great room. She'd earned her first major timeout there, too, after she'd taken a red crayon to the wall.

Sheila had used their budding Picasso's artwork as justification for not only repainting, but redecorating the entire room. As he had throughout the house, Dawson had given his late wife free rein. So, it was no surprise that everything reflected her preference for muted hues and soft fabrics. He'd never had a problem with the décor, but perhaps it was time for a change. He recalled the bold color choices in Eve's small loft apartment. Maybe something along those lines.

Especially in the bedroom.

Upstairs, he stood at the side of the bed they had shared last night. Eve had straightened the covers and replaced the duvet they had kicked off at some point during their lovemaking. He fished the pillow she'd used out from the bedding and brought it to his face. He could smell her perfume. It haunted him. *She* haunted him. The woman was on his mind, under his skin. She had been since their first meeting and that was especially the case now that he had made love to her.

He sank down on the side of the bed with a groan, recalling just how soft her skin had felt, how responsive she had been to his touch, how smug her smile had been when she'd curled up against his side afterward.

Dawson had worried he would regret making love to her. Not the actual act, but the fulfillment and sense of completion it brought. Surprisingly, he hadn't and he still didn't. He had meant it when he'd told her that he'd been intimate with no one since the accident. Guilt had always managed to quell any sexual desire he felt. But he hadn't felt guilty with Eve. In fact, even when he'd awakened with her beside him in the bed he'd shared with Sheila, under the very covers his late wife had picked out, he hadn't felt guilty. No. He'd felt happy and optimistic and eager not only to start the day, but to end it... with Eve.

For the first time in three long years, Dawson had felt truly alive. And *that* was what had stoked his guilt into a blazing bonfire.

Thinking back to their earlier conversation in the kitchen, he knew he had botched things horribly when he'd tried to keep Eve from reading too much into their lovemaking. *Temporary.* Was that really how he wanted things to be?

He recalled the way her happy expression had clouded over, even though she had managed to rally admirably. She wasn't the sort to stay down for long. Or, more likely, she wasn't the sort to *let* someone see her down.

He'd hurt her. Of all his many regrets, that was by far the biggest.

By midafternoon, he couldn't stand to be alone in

his house any longer. He considered going to Burke Financial. He'd spent more than one Saturday ensconced behind the desk in his office scouring spreadsheets and tracking market trends. But burying himself in work today held zero appeal. Another option did. Before he could change his mind, he called for his driver.

"Where to?" Jonas asked through the lowered window that partitioned the front seat from the back.

"I'm not sure," Dawson admitted while securing his seatbelt. "By any chance, do you know a store where I can buy a nice pair of women's boots?"

Eve toed off the practical if unattractive pair of rubber ankle boots she had fished from the back of her closet when she'd briefly stopped at her apartment after leaving Dawson's. She'd been home only long enough to change into a new outfit and pull her hair into a ponytail before heading to the nearest mall. Now it was nearly six o'clock, and she was starving and exhausted. She pulled off her jacket and scarf and tossed them across the back of her couch. She'd hang them up later. Right now, she needed something to eat.

She pulled the chicken breast from her fridge. She could butterfly it, pound it flat and then sauté it in a little olive oil with some minced garlic and Italian spices. If the lettuce in the crisper hadn't wilted, she could make herself a salad to go with it. Meal plan decided, she got to work. She was beating the chicken with a kitchen mallet when the doorbell chimed.

Eve expected to find a deliveryman in the hallway. Packages were arriving daily. But when she opened the door, meat mallet still in one hand, it was Dawson who stood there.

"Hello, Eve."

"I wasn't expecting you," she said.

"Is that why you're holding a weapon?"

She glanced at her raised hand and laughed as she lowered it. "It's for the chicken."

"What did the chicken do?" he asked.

"Funny. Come on in. I was just making something to eat. I'm willing to share."

"Thanks, but I won't stay long. I just came to drop this off."

He held out the package that had been tucked under his arm. The large rectangular box was expertly wrapped in festive paper. The top sported a large and equally festive-looking bow, which was slightly crushed now.

"What's this?" she asked.

"You'll have to open it to find out."

"It's for me?" She blinked. For a moment she had thought, hoped even, that Dawson had decided to do a little of his Christmas shopping on his own. The notion had pleased her, even if it would cut into her commission. But a gift for her? She wasn't sure how she felt about that given the perplexing nature of their relationship.

Dawson nodded. "Your name is on the tag. Unless I've got the wrong Eve Hawley." He started to pull the package away.

"Oh, no. You've got the right one. And I happen to love surprises. Just give me a minute to wash my hands."

She quickly put the chicken away, scrubbed her hands and returned to find him still standing just inside the closed door.

"Hey, take your coat off and come sit down," she told him as she took a seat on the couch.

He handed her the package and took off his coat, which he draped across the back of the couch with hers. Eve waited until he was seated to give the package a shake. She couldn't stop a smile from curving her lips.

"I wonder what it could be."

"Only one way to find out," he said.

Without another word, she shredded the paper. She recognized the logo on the box immediately and was laughing even before she lifted the top.

"You bought me boots."

"I said I would. I'm a man of my word," Dawson said.

"I can't believe you remembered the brand and

style." She checked the side of the box then and chuckled in amazement. "And my size."

"You're not the only one who's good with details." But then Dawson cleared his throat and admitted, "Actually, I got lucky on the size."

"Well, thank you." She leaned over and kissed him on the cheek.

"You're welcome."

He didn't move, but Eve did. She set the boots aside and gave in to temptation. By the time the next kiss ended she was on his lap, straddling him.

"Well..." he said.

"Uh-huh."

"I..."

"Yeah. Me, too."

"We're not talking in full sentences." He laughed.

"We are now. So, is Jonas downstairs?"

He glanced at his watch. "For another three minutes. I told him if I didn't return in fifteen, he could leave and I'd call him when I needed him to come back."

"Hedging your bets?" she asked.

"I wasn't sure you'd be home or, for that matter, that you would want to see me."

"So, if you leave right now, you'll still have a ride?"

He nodded. "Well, unless I take the elevator and get stuck between floors."

"The elevator got fixed yesterday."

"You mean I took the stairs for nothing?"

"I wouldn't say nothing," she replied, nipping at his lower lip.

"So, do you think I should stay?" he asked.

When the corners of her mouth lifted in a smile, his followed suit. By the time this kiss ended, she had relieved him of his shirt and he was in the process of returning the favor.

"Loft?" he asked, his breath sawing in and out of his chest.

"Couch. We're already here."

"I love it when you're practical," he murmured against her mouth.

After that, neither one of them wasted either time or energy on words.

A while later, it had grown dark in the apartment until the table lamp clicked on thanks to an automatic timer. Dawson felt Eve rouse beside him a moment before she untangled her legs from his and got to her feet. She grabbed his coat from the back of the couch to cover herself. She presented a sexy picture despite his conservative black wool. Her hair was a gorgeously tousled mess, her eye makeup smudged in a way that gave her eyes a smoky appearance. But she looked uncertain.

He knew how she felt.

"I wasn't planning this when I came here today," he told her quietly. It was important that she knew that. This hadn't been intended as some casual booty call.

"I know. That's what makes it special." She glanced behind her toward the kitchen area. "I suppose I should play the hostess and ask if you'd like something to eat or drink."

He felt chilled now that she wasn't beside him on the couch, but he made no effort to cover his nakedness. "You wouldn't happen to have hot cocoa with little marshmallows? For some reason I have a real craving for that."

"Sorry. No marshmallows." She shrugged. "No milk either for that matter. I never made it to the grocery store this week despite my good intentions."

He sat up and reached for his clothes, which were scattered about on the floor with hers. "You're a personal shopper, Eve."

She lifted her shoulders in a shrug. "And the cobbler's children have no shoes."

"Right." He laughed. "I won't ask how you're coming on your own Christmas shopping."

"Good, because I haven't started it. Luckily, I don't have much to do. My list is pretty short."

Dressed in his jeans, he followed her into the kitchen. He didn't bother with his shirt. She was still wearing his coat... and nothing else. Since she didn't have any cocoa, she uncorked a bottle of wine and poured them each a glass.

"Will you be going back East to spend the holidays with family?" he asked.

Eve leaned against the counter and sipped her wine.

"No. I'm staying here."

But you'll be alone, he almost said. Which would have been rich coming from him since that was exactly how he intended to spend his holiday.

Eve was saying, "I have no reason to make the trip back East. My dad is on the road, and I don't really have any extended family that I feel especially close to these days."

The matter-of-fact way she said it caused his chest to ache.

"What about the relatives who helped raise you after your mom died and your dad left?"

"They haven't exactly gone out of their way to make me feel welcome since I moved out. I dropped in once for Christmas while I was still in college, but it was awkward. My cousin was engaged and everyone was fawning over his fiancée and how she was going to be the perfect addition to their family. I felt like I was intruding."

"I'm sure you weren't," he said, although he knew no such thing. But it bothered him too much to think otherwise.

"I don't know. They had even hung a stocking for

her on the mantle, but mine wasn't there. Anyway, I haven't heard from them in years. Since college I've mainly spent my holidays with friends."

Or boyfriends, he thought, recalling Drew.

"Will you get together with Carole? I know the two of you have gotten close."

"I'll see her a couple of days before Christmas," Eve replied. "We're meeting for breakfast so we can exchange gifts, and then I'm driving her to the airport. She's visiting with her sister in Seattle until after the first of the year."

"What about your father? I know you said he's on the road, but maybe you two could meet up somewhere," Dawson suggested, hoping for a more satisfactory response than he had gotten so far. But he knew from the way she rolled her eyes that he wasn't going to like what she had to say.

"Not likely. I got a postcard from him earlier this month. He's playing at a pub in Galveston through the New Year. He sent me a lovely Laura Ashley-print dress. The pattern is very similar to the wallpaper in your downstairs powder room."

"Floral? You?"

Dawson's incredulous reaction brought a smile to her lips.

"Yes. I'm not big on flower prints, but then my father doesn't know me well enough to have figured that out."

His heart squeezed painfully once again.

"So, what will you do?" he asked.

"I could take it back. Whoever he talked into buying it included a gift receipt in the card. More likely, though, I'll donate it to charity." She shrugged. "It's a nice dress, even if it's not my style."

"That's not what I meant, Eve. Where will you go for Christmas?"

"Nowhere. I'll celebrate here. I'm going to put up a tree this week." She glanced toward the main living space. "Nothing big, but I want it to be real, you know? I haven't had a real tree in a long time. Drew was allergic."

Dawson frowned. "I guess I just assumed..."

"What? That you were the only one who would be spending Christmas alone?"

"Sorry."

"No, I am. Let's forget that." She raised her glass, inadvertently offering a tantalizing glimpse of flesh beneath his coat. "I saved this Chianti for a special occasion. I'd say this is special."

"I think so, too."

Their glasses clinked together before they sipped the wine. Then Dawson said, "I know it's late, but there's an all-night diner about twenty minutes from here. Want to go?"

"Gee, that chicken breast in my fridge is going to start feeling neglected," she teased. "But if you're offering to take me out to dinner, you won't find me playing hard to get."

"Good. I'll call my driver. Tell him to give us an hour."

"We don't need to bother Jonas," she protested. "My Tahoe is parked just up the block."

"It's no bother," Dawson objected. "It's what the man is paid to do."

"Go ahead and call him," she said, but then added, "And tell him to take the rest of the night off."

"How will I get home?" he asked, his heart picking up speed.

"I can take you later," she said.

"Oh?" He stepped closer.

"Or not," she added, letting his coat slip off one shoulder. "I know how you like to make plans, Dawson, but how about we play that one by ear?"

He set aside his wine and moved closer so that he could kiss her bare shoulder. "You know, I'm beginning to like spontaneity."

"I can tell." She sighed and set her wine aside so she could reach for him. As their bodies came together, his coat fell to the floor.

Dawson stayed the night with Eve and not just because he had dismissed his driver and it seemed wrong to ask her to drive him home on such a cold night. No. He had wanted to remain in her cozy home, in the life-affirming warmth of her presence. It had nothing to do with sex—as incredible and satisfying as that was—and everything to do with the woman. Eve was like a crackling fire to a pair of cold hands, beckoning him to reach out and warm himself.

His heart was definitely starting to thaw. The prospect terrified him because he recognized just how deep his feelings for Eve went. In a very short time, she had gone from being a stranger and pesky contract employee, to the very center of his life. Everything seemed to revolve around her. He wasn't sure what he had to offer her, but he knew he didn't want to lose her. He couldn't lose her.

It came as a shock when Dawson realized he had only felt this way about one other woman in his life.

And he'd married her.

CHAPTER TWELVE

When Dawson awoke the next morning, the soundtrack to *Les Misérables* was playing. He hunted around the loft for his shirt, but then remembered he'd left it by the couch. Pulling on his jeans, he padded downstairs. He found her at the kitchen counter. Last night, the sight of her in his coat had made him crazy. This morning, she was wearing his shirt, its tail barely covering her nicely rounded butt, and measuring grounds into the coffeemaker.

She took his groan to mean something else. "This will be done in a minute," she said over her shoulder.

"No hurry. My shirt looks good on you." He came up behind her, settled his hands on her hips, and nuzzled the side of her neck.

"Mmm." Eve issued a throaty sigh. "I live for caffeine, but I could forgo my morning pot of coffee if I got to wake up to this every day."

He felt her stiffen after she said it and then she turned. "Sorry. I hope that didn't make you uncomfortable."

"No." And it hadn't. Actually, he found the scenario her words conjured up quite appealing.

But she was uncomfortable. That was clear when she added, "I don't want you to think we need to go through the whole this-is-temporary discussion again."

"I don't." And he meant it.

The soundtrack came to Fantine's heart-wrenching solo about the life she'd once dreamed of having and the man who'd used and discarded her. It wasn't the ideal song for lightening the mood, but Dawson attempted to do that by saying, "How about a dance while we wait for our coffee? This time, I'll lead."

"Okay. Show me your moves, John Travolta." Her throaty laughter echoed in the lofted space.

Dawson wiped the smile off her face by spinning her out and then around in a circle.

"Nice," she said once she was back in his arms. "Have you got any others?"

"An entire repertoire."

"Really? Are they all as good as that last one?" she asked with an arch of one brow.

"Better."

Her dark eyes glittered. "Well, then, by all means, show me."

None of his moves would have won a dance competition, but they were a little fancier than the standard steps.

"Not bad," she told him when the song ended. "Maybe I will let you lead the next time we dance in public."

"Not bad? What do you think of this?" He levered her backward over his arm until her torso was nearly parallel to the kitchen floor. The drama of the move was mitigated by the fact that they had both begun to laugh.

"I said show me, not show off and throw both our backs out in the process."

Oddly, his back felt perfectly fine. And his shoulders and neck, which were usually tight to the point of going into spasms, were pain-free and almost relaxed.

"Sorry. I couldn't resist doing that," Dawson said as he brought her upright.

Eve stayed in his arms, her hands flat on his bare chest, her hips flush against his. "What else can't you resist?" she asked.

"I think you know."

"Tell me anyway," she whispered.

"You."

By the time they had both showered and dressed, the morning was spent. The *Les Mis* soundtrack was playing again when Dawson joined Eve in the living room. She was sitting on the sofa with one foot perched on the small round table in front of her. He groaned when he realized what she was doing: painting her toenails.

Red.

"I just made a fresh pot of coffee. The mugs are in the cupboard next to the sink. Help yourself," she told him without sparing him a glance.

When he didn't move, she stopped what she was doing and looked up. "Everything okay?"

"I've got this thing for red toenails."

Her lips twitched. "On women or is there something you want to tell me?"

"On women in general, but on *you* in particular," he clarified.

"Sounds like a fetish."

"I guess you could call it that," he agreed as he took a seat in the chair opposite the couch.

She pointed the small brush from the polish bottle in his direction. "You know, when we first met, I wouldn't have figured you for the fetish sort."

"Why not?" he asked, amused.

She wrinkled her nose. "Are you kidding? You were much, much too uptight and controlling."

"Uptight and controlling people can't have fetishes?" he asked, intrigued by her logic, even if he found her description of him somewhat insulting.

"It's pretty hard to give into your longings when you live by a rigid set of rules."

As usual, he was enjoying their banter. The woman had him coiled in crazy knots and she thought he was inflexible. "So, you think I'm unyielding?"

"No." Then she clarified. "Well, not anymore."

"What changed your mind?"

"I don't think my mind has changed as much as you've changed. You've loosened up, Dawson. A lot."

Eve went back to painting her nails. Dawson, meanwhile, found he was grateful to be seated since her answer floored him.

If what she said was true, then Eve was responsible.

She had finished painting her toes and was putting the cap back on the polish, when he found his voice again. "I didn't loosen up. *You* loosened me up. You've been good for me, Eve. You are a rare and truly unexpected gift."

It was the season for gifts, both getting and giving. Dawson had long stopped caring about either. Or so he'd thought. Across from him, he watched Eve's eyes grow bright.

"That's quite a compliment. I don't know that I deserve it, but thank you."

"You do deserve it." He swallowed. "You deserve a hell of a lot more than that."

Sadness leaked into her smile when she replied, "So do you, Dawson."

He opened his mouth to disagree, but his standard arguments suddenly didn't seem to fit. In the background, the persecuted Jean Valjean sang out his name and prisoner number, determined to stop running from the intrepid and intractable Inspector Javert. Eve was still smiling. She was so lovely, so loving and alive. Maybe, Dawson thought, it was time for him to stop running from his past, too.

It was just after four when Eve drove Dawson home. They were halfway to his house when he said unexpectedly, "Get in the right lane."

"What? Why," she asked, even as she flicked on her blinker.

"Take the next exit. I'm getting hungry."

Before driving him home, they had walked up the block to her favorite Chinese restaurant and eaten what Eve considered her main meal of the day, so his reply surprised her.

"How can you be hungry? We ate less than an hour ago," she reminded him.

"It was all the exercising we did." He winked.

She liked Dawson like this. Light-hearted, seemingly carefree. She'd meant it when she'd told him he had changed. Looking at him now, she saw very little of the lost and lonely man who had barely tolerated her many questions.

She took the exit he indicated, but didn't see any restaurants right off the highway, except for the usual fast-food joints.

"Where are we going?" she asked.

He compounded the mystery with his cryptic, "You'll see."

Eve followed his directions, turning right at the traffic light and then left three streets later. They wound up in a high-end residential neighborhood where the houses were older and exuded elegance and charm. Almost all of them were decorated for the holidays. In the fading daylight, shimmering light bulbs glowed along the eaves and followed the steep peaks of the rooflines.

"Pull over here," he said, pointing just ahead.

They stopped in front of a gorgeous home that sported a full-sized manger and Nativity scene in its huge front yard. She had a good idea where they were even before he told her, "This is where I grew up."

"Do you want me to drop you off?" Her heart swelled. His parents were going to be so happy to see him.

But he said, "No, Eve. I want you to join me for Sunday dinner with my family."

"I... really?" It seemed a big step, even given how much he had changed between them.

"Yes."

Vanity made Eve look in the rearview mirror. "I'm a mess. I wish you had said something earlier. I'm wearing yoga pants. And my hair—"

"Is fine. You look beautiful," he assured her, reaching out for her hand when she started to fuss with her curls. "There's no dress code, Eve. It's just my family."

Yes, but outfitted in designer clothes, her hair done and her makeup fully applied, she would have more confidence. Her gaze cut to the impressive home. It was Tudor-style, easily five thousand square feet, with a lawn that seemed as long as a football field. Drew's family had lived in a similarly elegant house. The old vulnerability crept in.

"I don't belong here," she whispered.

"Eve?"

She cleared her throat, tried again. "They're not expecting me, Dawson."

"Sunday dinner is a standing invitation," he said.

"For you."

"And for whomever I choose to bring as my guest." He glanced away. "And you're the first guest I've brought since the accident."

Which was exactly why his invitation meant so much to her. Still, she asked, "Are you sure your mother won't mind me tagging along?"

"Not at all. You were at the charity ball. The more the merrier is her motto. Besides, there is always enough food on Sundays to feed half the neighborhood." He held out a hand. "So, what do you say, Eve?"

Banishing the last of her doubts, she nodded. "I'd love to."

Dawson's family didn't regard Eve from a respectable distance as they had the night of the charity ball. They quite literally mobbed her the moment she and Dawson entered the foyer, welcoming him home and welcoming her into their midst with hugs and handshakes, laughter and boisterous greetings.

Dawson watched Eve soak it all in. Despite her earlier hesitation, she seemed to take his family's enthusiastic welcome in stride. He wasn't sure what had made him tell her to take the exit for his parents' home when they were on the highway. But he was glad he had followed his instinct.

"Christmas came early. I'm so glad you're here," his mother enthused. Tallulah wrapped him in a hug and whispered into his ear, "And I'm so glad you brought Eve."

"I am, too," Dawson replied honestly as he hugged her back.

"Does this mean you'll be here for Christmas?" she asked as he began to pull away.

Amid the ongoing commotion, Dawson pretended not to hear her.

CHAPTER THIRTEEN

Christmas Eve was the day after next, but Dawson had not begun to pack for his trip. Usually by this point, he had at least worked up a list of summer clothes for Ingrid to wash and press, if need be, but he hadn't done even that. He'd been too busy.

With Eve.

They had spent nearly every evening together since having dinner with his parents. For that matter, they had also spent nearly every night wrapped in each other's arms, warm and worn-out from their lovemaking.

The start of a new year was just over a week away, and Dawson felt a sense of anticipation that had been lacking since the accident. And that remained so even with the anniversary of the crash looming like a large thundercloud.

Tonight, he and Eve were meeting with his

friends Tony and Christine for dinner at the steak restaurant they'd mentioned wanting to try at the charity ball. The other couple had been surprised when he'd called them earlier in the week to see if they were free. He had the feeling they had shuffled around plans to accommodate him. If so, he was grateful. He was especially grateful that after all the times he had brushed them off, they hadn't given up on their friendship.

The four of them chatted nonstop through all three courses of the meal. Dawson and Sheila had spent many wonderful evenings in this couple's company. Tonight, the dynamic was different, as was so much of Dawson's life these days. But they were not only polite to Eve, he could tell they genuinely liked her. He also could tell that the feeling was mutual.

"Well, I hate to break up the party, but we still have some last-minute shopping to do for the kids," Christine said, laying her napkin aside.

Tony was reaching for his wallet, but Dawson stopped him.

"This was my idea, so it's my treat."

"Okay, thanks. We'll get the check the next time," Tony replied meaningfully.

"I'll hold you to it," Dawson said.

After they left, Dawson and Eve stayed for a second cup of coffee. It had been a wonderful evening, but the night was still young, and he was eager to get her alone.

"Ready to go?" he asked.

"Yes."

While Dawson went to retrieve their checked coats, Eve excused herself to use the ladies' room. After applying fresh lipstick, she returned to the small lobby area just as a petite blonde woman came up behind Dawson and tapped his shoulder. Something about her seemed familiar to Eve.

"Hey, stranger," the young woman said when he turned. Then she threw her arms around and hugged him. "It's good to see you."

"Natasha, hello." He looked startled as he pulled out of her embrace. But beyond that, Eve had a hard time gauging his expression.

"Mom and Dad are in the lounge having a drink. We're a little early for our reservation," the woman explained.

"How are your parents?" Eve heard him ask.

"They're doing well, all things considered." Even in profile, Eve could tell the woman's smile was strained. "You know how it is. This time of year, especially."

"Yes."

"How are you doing?" She tipped her head to one side as she studied him.

"I'm fine."

"Come on, Dawson. No need for the stiff-upper-lip routine around me."

"I'm fine, Nat, really." He glanced past her then and his gaze connected with Eve's. "I'm doing much better."

"You've told me that before. But you know what, I almost believe you this time. You look good, Dawson. Happy. Almost like your old self."

Eve could see him swallow. "I'm getting there. And what about you?"

She shrugged. "I have good days and bad days. More good than bad now. So, I suppose that's progress."

He squeezed her arm. "I'm glad to hear that, Nat."

"It took a while," she admitted. "But I suppose I should warn you that Mom's not quite there yet."

He nodded solemnly. "I figured as much."

"That's not your concern, though. I know she said some awful, hurtful things to you right after the accident and then at the funeral that made you feel, well, responsible, but it was her grief talking."

"I'm still sorry—"

"Don't be." She cut him off. Then her expression brightened. "So, who are you here with?"

Dawson extended his hand to Eve, beckoning her forward.

"I'd like you to meet Eve Hawley. Eve, this is Natasha Derringer, Sheila's sister."

Eve had figured out the young woman's identity already. "Hello," she said, shaking Natasha's hand.

"Dawson's a wonderful man. The best." Natasha sent him a warm smile. "It's nice to see him out and looking happy again." The young woman's eyes were bright, her tone sincere.

Eve was so taken aback by the heartfelt sentiment, she could only smile.

"I'm so glad I ran into you. *Both* of you," Natasha enthused.

It was the perfect ending to a perfect evening, Eve decided, until everything went sideways with the appearance of Natasha's parents, who followed the hostess out of the lounge. Apparently, their table was ready.

"Give us a minute," the older man said, dismissing the hostess.

He gave Dawson a friendly clap on the back, but the dour-looking woman beside him said nothing. Her silence was damning.

"Clayton, Angela," Dawson said, his tone strained. "It's good to see you. How are you both?"

"We're doing all right." Clayton bobbed his graying head. "You know how it is."

"Yes."

Sheila's mother, however, barely acknowledged

Dawson before rudely staring off in the opposite direction.

"Mom, Dad, this is Dawson's friend, Eve Hawley," Natasha inserted into the awkward pause.

Dawson finished the introductions. "Eve, this is Angela and Clayton Derringer."

"Hello. It's nice to meet you."

Everyone sensed the awkwardness of the moment. Everyone seemed determined to make the best of it. Everyone except Angela. While Clayton greeted Eve with a polite smile, the older woman glared at her with unmistakable contempt and snubbed her attempt to shake hands. Afterward, she rounded on Dawson and released her venom.

"How nice for you, Dawson, that you are able to go on with your life," she drawled. "You've moved on with someone new, and now you're out acting as if my daughter never existed. As if your own daughter never existed."

"Angela," Clayton began at the same time a horrified Natasha said, "Mom, please. That's not fair."

"Fair? Two people are dead because of this man."

Eve gasped. Clayton and Natasha looked mortified. Dawson, meanwhile, pulled back as if he'd been slapped.

"I can assure you. I haven't forgotten either Sheila or Isabelle. I never will."

He'd been holding Eve's hand. But he released it as he spoke. In that instant, it was as if their emotional connection had been broken. Witnessing his withdrawal, part of Eve broke, too. The funny, fun-loving man she had spent more than a week with was no more. The remote and intractable Dawson Burke she'd first met stood in his place.

After a round of apologies, none of which was offered by Angela, the Derringers went in search of the hostess, and Eve and Dawson headed out to the parking lot. He helped her into the limo's rear seat, but instead of joining her, he sat opposite her. The drive home was unbearably quiet. When they reached her apartment building, it came as no surprise when Dawson told Jonas to wait for him while he walked Eve to her door.

"You're not staying tonight." It was issued as a statement rather than a question as the elevator climbed to her floor.

"No."

"Are we still on for dinner tomorrow evening?" she made herself ask him.

She knew the answer even before he said, "Sorry, but I'm going to have to cancel."

The elevator doors slid open and they both stepped out. "Did something come up?"

"I've got some loose ends I need to clear up before the holidays." They had reached her apartment door. He took the key from her hand and slid it into the lock. As he turned it, he added, "I also have some packing to do."

Eve felt mule-kicked. "For Cabo?"

"Yes."

"You're going."

"You knew that I was," he said defensively as they stepped into her apartment.

"I guess I'd hoped you had changed your mind and had decided to spend the holidays with loved ones."

"Christmas isn't a holiday for me, Eve. It's the anniversary of my wife and daughter's deaths. I have nothing to celebrate." The words came out forcefully, angrily.

And he wouldn't have anything to celebrate as long as that was his focus.

"I won't pretend to know how you feel, Dawson. My mother was thoughtful enough to die on a day that didn't hold any other special meaning for me. But I do know how your family feels. They didn't just lose Sheila and Isabelle on that Christmas Eve three years ago. They lost you. Just as I lost my dad the day my mother overdosed."

"I'm sorry, Eve."

"I am, too. I'm sorry for my dad that, in addition to missing out on so much of my life, he's missed out on so much of his own. He's not a happy man. Are you happy?"

"I don't deserve—"

"Deserve to be happy?" she finished for him. Frustration and more than a little anger leaked into her tone when she said, "Oh, please! Stop playing the pity card. It's gotten old. They died. You lived. Deal with it!" she shouted. She moderated her tone as much as she could to add, "Because in making yourself pay, you are also making everyone who loves you pay. I'm not just talking about your family now, Dawson."

"No, Eve." He shook his head, looking miserable. "Don't love me."

"That's not something you can dictate or control. I love you, Dawson. It's a done deed. I said it. And I'm not taking it back."

He stumbled back a step. It was sadly apropos that he was now on one side of the threshold and she was on the other. "I'm going, Eve."

"Of course, you are." She expelled a breath then, acceptance taking the place of her anger. "Wait. I have something for you. Something that I had planned to give you on Christmas morning, but since it doesn't look like I'll be seeing you then, I guess I'll give it to you now."

"You didn't need to buy me anything," he protested.

"I wanted to."

"I have something for you, too, but obviously I didn't bring it with me tonight."

No, because before the run-in with Sheila's mother in the restaurant, he had planned to see her again.

"That's all right."

She turned to get his gift from its hiding place in the console table next to the door. Her heart was all the heavier when Dawson remained in the hallway, as if eager to make his escape.

"It's not much," she told him, handing him the small package. "It's one of those it's-the-thought-that-counts type gifts."

"Well, thank you."

When he started to peel back the paper, she stopped him.

"Don't open it now. Wait until Christmas morning."

"Okay." With a nod, he tucked the present into the pocket of his overcoat. "Speaking of Christmas, my parents usually eat dinner around three in the afternoon. I know you would be more than welcome there. They would love to see you."

They would love to see Dawson even more, but all Eve said was, "Thanks, but I don't think so. I'd feel... awkward."

He frowned. "What will you do then?"

"I'll celebrate here." And she would. It was what she had planned to do before her relationship with Dawson had turned intimate. "I'm going to pick out a tree tomorrow. Once I bring it home, I'm going to string some lights and garland around it, and douse it with a boatload of tinsel."

"And then what?" he asked.

"I have a new recipe I want to try. I'm going to the grocery store tomorrow to get all the ingredients. I'm planning a major feast. I'll be eating leftovers through New Year's." She forced out a laugh. "After that, I'll put on my pajamas and watch *It's a Wonderful Life*."

"Eve, you don't have to spend Christmas alone," he said.

"Neither do you. We all have choices, Dawson." She stepped out into the hallway and rose on tiptoe to kiss his cheek. "Merry Christmas."

He was still standing there when she closed the door in his frowning face.

Dawson was in a nasty mood. He blamed Eve for that. She was trying to make him feel guilty, he decided. Yes, that was it. She had known he would be leaving town for the holidays. He had never made her any promises.

Nor had she asked for any, his conscience reminded him. Even when they had laid in bed, wrapped in one another's arms while sharing their innermost thoughts, she hadn't asked Dawson about the future.

Temporary.

That was the adjective she had applied to their relationship at the very beginning. More accurately, it was what she assumed he'd intended. And he had let the assumption go unchallenged, even though as the days passed and their relationship began to feel far more permanent.

We all have choices, Dawson.

On Christmas Eve day, he left the office just after one in the afternoon. The company party was scheduled for five o'clock, but he wouldn't be there. He had a flight to catch at six. Mrs. Stern would see to it that the bonuses were distributed to his employees, just as she had seen to it that the gifts Eve had purchased for his clients had been wrapped and delivered.

As for the gifts for his family, Jonas would take those over. Dawson called his mother from his cell on the drive home to tell her about his plans. He'd purposely put it off, neither confirming nor declining. As he'd expected, Talulah wasn't pleased with his decision, and she let him know it in no uncertain terms. Dawson wasn't able to get a word in edgewise for the first ten minutes of their conversation.

Finally, he managed, "I'm really sorry if there was a mix-up, Mom."

He heard her sigh and imagined her pacing the length of the kitchen when she replied. "Well, I hope you and Eve have a good time in Cabo. We'll make plans to get together after the holidays. Be sure to wish Eve a merry Christmas for us."

"Mom, about that, Eve's not coming with me."

"What? You're going alone? But I thought..." Her

words trailed off before she added, "The way you look at her, Dawson. The way she looks at you. It's as plain as can be that you're falling in love with her. Your dad and I are so happy you're finally moving on."

"No!" His shout caused Jonas to glance over his shoulder. Dawson lowered his voice and moderated his tone. "I like Eve, but..."

"But what?"

He glommed onto the first excuse he could think of. "We hardly know one another."

The explanation rang hollow even to his own ears. The length of their acquaintance had nothing to do with his feelings for Eve.

Sure enough, his mother pointed this out. "I fell in love with your father on our first date. He waited until we had been seeing one another for six months before he finally proposed, but he said he had known I was the one for him as soon as he laid eyes on me. That girl is special, Dawson."

"Sheila was special."

"Thinking Eve is, too, doesn't change that." When he was silent, his mother added, "Sheila was special. But she's gone, son. Please don't stay so mired in the past that you let Eve get away."

Because his eyes had begun to sting, he closed them. "Things between the two of us probably aren't going to work out the way you're hoping, Mom."

Talulah made a humming sound. "Don't worry

about me. Ask yourself this, Dawson. Are they going to work out the way you were hoping?"

After he ended the call, he stared out the window at the mid-afternoon traffic. When he shifted in his seat, something in his pocket bit into his side. He reached into his overcoat and pulled out the wrapped box. The gift Eve had given him the other day. He'd forgotten to take it out.

She had told him to open it on Christmas morning, but he was feeling so miserable at the moment, he decided not to wait. He peeled back the paper and lifted the small box's lid. She had told him the gift fell into the it's-the-thought-that-counts category. Well, her thoughtfulness left him stunned.

She had given him, the man who had boycotted Christmas for the past three years, a small glass ornament in the shape of two embracing angels. He pulled out the note tucked inside the box and read it.

Dear Dawson,

This is for your tree. Hang these angels on the highest branch and, when you're feeling sad, take time to celebrate Sheila and Isabelle's lives and remember the love and laughter you shared.

Love, Eve

. . .

Dawson swallowed. He didn't have a tree. He hadn't put one up since the accident. But fifteen minutes later when the limo rolled to a stop in his curved driveway, he realized Eve had thought of that, too. Two men were holding what looked to be a ten-foot-tall blue spruce as Ingrid stood on the porch wringing her hands.

"I explained to them that you're going out of town and that you certainly would not have ordered a Christmas tree," his flustered housekeeper said when he reached them.

"It's all right. I'll handle this." And even though Dawson was a man of action, a man used to making decisions, he stood rooted in place, staring at the tree for several long minutes.

"Hey, mister, are you going to tell us where you want this or what?" one of the delivery men finally asked. "We've got another half-dozen deliveries to make yet today."

Take it back.

That was what he should say. It made the most sense. He was leaving. He had neither the time nor the inclination to decorate it. And a live tree would be a fire hazard. But as his thumb stroked over the delicate ornament that was still cupped in the palm of his hand, the words that came out of his mouth were, "It's time to let go."

He didn't need to let go of the memories, he realized, rather the misplaced guilt and anger and all the other negative emotions that had kept him from not only living but remembering Sheila and Isabelle as anything more than victims. There had been so much more to the life they'd shared than the death that separated them.

Eve, his sweet and lovely Eve, had known that.

"You want us to let go of this thing?" The man looked incredulous.

The comment startled a laugh from Dawson. "No. Take it in the house." He called for Ingrid then. When she returned to the porch, he told her, "Show them to the great room. I think the tree would look best in the corner by the big window."

And with that, Dawson strode to the home's four-car garage.

CHAPTER FOURTEEN

It had been three years since Dawson had last driven a vehicle of any make or model. The accident had totaled his luxury four-door sedan. His insurance company had paid to replace it, but Dawson had never been behind the wheel of the new car. For the most part, it had remained in the garage, except on the occasions Jonas took it out for regular maintenance.

Parked on the other side of the car was the limousine he'd purchased when he'd hired his driver. Jonas was probably in his rooms upstairs. Dawson liked the size of the limo. Buckled into the center of the rear seat, he'd always been able to beat back the worst of his fear by using the commute time to read *The Wall Street Journal* or make business calls.

He divided his gaze between the two vehicles. The limo's interior would still be warm from the drive home. He could summon Jonas, who could be downstairs and ready to leave in no time. But the keys to the sedan were hanging on the hook by the door. Dawson sucked in a breath and came to a decision.

Once he was seated inside the car, he hung the angel ornament from the rearview mirror. His hands shook as he buckled himself in. A seat belt, an airbag, and divine intervention had saved his life three years ago, or so he had overheard one of the rescue workers on the scene say that night. Dawson prayed for that same divine intervention now as he shifted out of park and inched the car out of the garage.

He kept to the side streets, driving slower than the posted speeds and testing the brakes more often than was necessary. The roads were clear, but he didn't want to take any chances. Forty minutes later, his confidence buoyed, he turned onto a busy four-lane, adjusting his speed to keep up with traffic. Finally, he decided to venture onto the highway. He bypassed the entrance ramp twice before he worked up the courage to turn down it. Thirty... forty... fifty... His heart rate accelerated along with the car. Then he was flipping on the blinker, merging into traffic, on his way to his future, assuming he wasn't too late. He gripped the steering wheel anxiously. Along the way, he would have to face his past.

A mile ahead was the spot where his life had changed and Sheila and Isabelle's lives had ended.

He had not driven past the site since then, even if that meant Jonas had to go out of their way to get where he needed to go. Dawson figured it made sense that he was the one behind the wheel for this moment.

He didn't stop as he approached the underpass, although he did slow down, forcing the cars behind him to brake and shift lanes. A couple drivers went around him, one blaring his horn and gesturing in irritation. Dawson didn't care. He barely spared the other man a glance. His attention was on the abutment. He waited to be assailed by grief and guilt and the horrible memories from that night. Before it came fully into view, he worried that once he saw the spot, he wouldn't be able to continue driving. What if he had to pull to the shoulder and call Jonas to come for him, and then have his car towed back to the house?

But none of that happened.

To his surprise, what had been the scene of horrible carnage three years earlier, now looked innocuous and nondescript. He felt sorrow as he drove past it, but sadness wasn't the only emotion. He also felt oddly free now that he had seen it, as if he'd been released from the self-recriminations that had held him hostage. The sun caught on the ornament, drawing his gaze to the rearview mirror. In it, the accident site grew smaller and his grieving heart grew lighter as he pressed the gas pedal and accelerated to keep up with traffic. He was, quite literally, moving on.

In his head he heard his mother asking if things between him and Eve were going to work out the way he had been hoping. This time he had an answer.

"If I have anything to say about it, they will," he said aloud.

One hour and one stop later, he arrived at Eve's apartment. Despite his earlier resolve, his legs felt a little shaky as he waited for her to answer his knock.

She opened the door wearing blue jeans and a sweatshirt. Her hair was pulled back in a ponytail. She wasn't holding a meat mallet this time, but she did have a twenty-dollar bill in her hand.

"Dawson." She blinked in surprise. "I thought you were the takeout guy."

He tried to gauge her reaction. Was she happy to see him? Angry? He couldn't tell.

"Can I come in?"

Christmas music played in the background and the scent of popcorn wafted out the door. It was a moment before she stepped back. "Sure."

A short, misshapen tree was in the far corner of the room, completely dwarfed by the high ceiling. She'd already decorated it with multi-colored lights and appeared to be in the process of stringing popcorn and cranberries for a garland.

"No tinsel?" he asked.

"This is more environmentally friendly," she replied, motioning toward her homemade garland.

"It looks like you could use the tree you had delivered to my house," he said.

She closed her eyes and let out a sigh. "I'm sorry about that. I tried to cancel the delivery, but when I called it was already too late. I had placed the order when I thought... Well, before."

He knew what she meant. Eve had placed the order when she thought they would be spending Christmas together.

"I also opened the gift you gave me," he admitted.

She grimaced. "I shouldn't have given you that the other night. I nearly chased you down the hallway afterward and asked for it back. If I've offended you, I'm sorry. It wasn't my intention. I just wanted you to know—"

"That it's okay to be alive."

She nodded.

Dawson walked around her to the couch and picked up the strand of popcorn and cranberries she had been making. As he studied it, he said, "I'm never going to feel one hundred percent festive this time of year, Eve."

"No one who knows what you've been through would expect you to be," she said.

"I loved my wife."

"Of course, you did. You always will."

"And my daughter." His voice grew hoarse. "It's

hard to imagine how deeply you can love another person until you have a child. All you want to do is protect them and keep them safe."

"Not even the most devoted parent can do that. Some things are outside your control," she said.

Eve's heart ached for Dawson. His emotions were so raw. She wanted to go to him, wrap her arms around him and ease some of his pain. But this was his journey. And it was one he had to make by himself.

So, she stood by and watched helplessly as he bowed his head and his shoulders began to shake. His cheeks were wet when he looked up, but when he spoke, his words gave her hope.

"Part of me knows that the accident wasn't my fault."

She did go to him then, unable to hold back from consoling him any longer. She gently brushed away his tears. Afterward, she framed his face in her hands. "The rest of you will come to accept it in time."

He was nodding as he reached for her hands and brought them to his lips for a kiss. Her heart hammered, but her voice was steady when she said, "I know Jonas is downstairs, but do you have time for a glass of wine before heading to the airport?"

He was still holding her hands, rubbing their

palms in that erotic way of his. "Actually, I drove here myself."

"You d-did?" she stammered in surprise. That was a big step for him. Huge. Especially on this day of all days.

"It was time." He kissed the backs of her hands again.

What else is it time for?

Eve wanted to ask, but she resisted the impulse. Instead, she said, "Since you're driving yourself, maybe wine isn't a good idea. I can make some hot cocoa. I even have little marshmallows. Got time for a cup?"

"Sure. I'm not in a hurry. I'm thinking of taking a later flight."

Something about the way he was watching her had Eve's heart knocking out an extra beat. "You are?"

"I am."

"How much later?" she asked.

"That depends."

Her throat was threatening to close, but she managed a hoarse, "On what?"

"On your answer to a question." But then he corrected himself. "It's really more of a proposal than a question. I've heard that Cabo can be very romantic. Sandy beaches, gorgeous sunsets. It doesn't sound like the kind of place a man should go alone."

"Are you asking me to go with you?"

She wanted Dawson to stay in Denver for Christmas so he could spend it with all the people who loved him, but at least the two of them would be together.

"I am. But not for Christmas. I want to spend the holidays here. With you and my family."

"I was hoping you'd say that." She sighed. "And Cabo?"

"I think it's the perfect place to start a new life. The perfect place for, say, a honeymoon."

Eve felt light-headed when he pulled a small box from his pocket. When the man had said proposal, had he meant *proposal?* With a capital P. "Are you asking me to marry you?"

"Not yet." Before she had a chance to decide if she was disappointed, he went on. "When I ask you to marry me, I want to do it right. This is too rushed and not at all romantic."

Was he kidding? She'd be the judge of that. She started to object, but he pressed a finger to her lips.

"I know we haven't known one another very long, but the way I feel about you..." He swallowed. "I didn't think I could feel this way again. I didn't think I *deserved* to feel again. I'm in love with you, Eve. I started falling in love with you the night of the charity ball."

"I think that was when I started falling, too," she admitted.

She kissed him. It would have lasted longer,

maybe even ended horizontally on her couch, but she had to know. "What's in the box?"

He chuckled as he held it out to her. "Go ahead and open it."

She slipped off the lid and peered inside, confused at first by the sight of the small, leafy green ball. Dawson pulled it out using the red satin ribbon that was affixed to its top.

"Mistletoe," she murmured, and eyed him quizzically.

He nodded. "It's a reminder that we have a standing date for December twenty-fifth. I want to spend every Christmas with you from this year forward. What do you say, Eve?"

"That sounds an awful lot like a proposal, and a pretty romantic one at that."

"Fine. It's not my best work, but it is a proposal. Well?"

"Yes!" Eve snatched the mistletoe from his fingers and raised it above their heads. "Kiss me already."

A LETTER FROM JACKIE

Dear Reader,

Merry Christmas! I hope you enjoyed meeting with Eve and Dawson. Eve is one of my favorite characters because she's not afraid to speak her mind. And that was exactly what Dawson needed to break free from his tragic past.

This year has been a busy one for me. I released five books, including this one. (You can find them all on Amazon.) All the books were previously published by Harlequin, but they required a surprising amount of updating to make them more relevant in 2023. The technology references alone were very dated. Of course, I also couldn't resist tweaking the stories. In some cases, including for this book, I did quite a bit of revising. I'm happy with the finished product, and I hope you are, too.

As for 2024, my goal is to release at least three more updated books from my backlist. Be sure to check my website, www.jackiebraun.com, for details on specific dates. You can also sign up for my newsletter there so you'll always be the first to know what I'm doing. And you can follow me on social media: www.facebook.com/jbfridline, www.instagram.com/jackiebraunfridline, www.twitter.com/JBFridline, www.goodreads.com/jackiebraun.

Wishing you a very merry Christmas and a blessed new year.

Jackie Braun

ALSO BY JACKIE BRAUN

Other books by Jackie Braun

It Happened in Cannes

The Trillium Series:
Book One: *Nobody's Business*
Book Two: *Unfinished Business*
Book Three: *Strictly Business*

Revenge Best Served Hot